LOVE'S FRAGILE FLAME

LOVE'S FRAGILE FLAME

Phyllis Caggiano

BETHANY HOUSE PUBLISHERS
MINNEAPOLIS, MINNESOTA 55438
A Division of Bethany Fellowship, Inc.

Copyright © 1984
Phyllis Caggiano
All Rights Reserved

Published by Bethany House Publishers
A Division of Bethany Fellowship, Inc.
6820 Auto Club Road, Minneapolis, MN 55438

Printed in the United States of America

Library of Congress Cataloging in Publication Data

Caggiano, Phyllis, 1938-
    Love's fragile flame.

    1. Great Britain-History-Mary I, 1553-1558-
Fiction. I. Title.
PS3553.A345L6   1984   813'.54   83-22454
ISBN 0-87123-582-X

In memory of
Doris Elizabeth Walters
my mother,
my sister in Christ

PHYLLIS CAGGIANO, born, raised and married in Arizona, now makes a home for her husband and five children in the town of Glendale. She began writing some years ago and has had articles published in various periodicals. Research and writing for her first book, *Love's Fragile Flame,* required six years and included a visit to England for further background information and descriptions. She and her husband are active in the North Phoenix Baptist Church.

Chapter One

BEFORE ROSE blamed God for what happened, she blamed nature. It had been the rain to begin with, she decided. If only there had been less rain. Then, if the sun had not come out on that particular day. . . .

The summer of the year of our Lord, 1555, had been the wettest Rose could remember. Even the old graybeards who sat wagging their tongues and warming their bones in the smithy had reckoned that this was the worst summer England had known in fifty years. Water stood a foot deep at the crossroads in the center of the village. Stunted corn lay rotting in the nearby fields. Each morning Derick would slog through the mud to the smithy, stoke his fire, and do what little work there was while Rose stayed in the cottage. Her main household duty throughout the summer seemed to be catching the stream of soot-streaked rainwater as it ran from the smoke hole in the roof, down a rafter, and into a jar. The rushes, newly strewn upon the floor last spring, were now blackened with mildew.

On the last morning of August, as Rose emptied the jar of rainwater, her brain seemed fuzzy with mildew. She carefully replaced the empty jar under the stream of water and sat down by the hearthfire, conscious of her swelling abdomen.

"Ah me, another cruel trick of nature," she said wistfully. Her first child, a son, was stillborn last winter. She had hoped not to conceive again until the next autumn so that the child would be born in a fair and pleasant month when fresh food would be plenteous and her milk would be rich and wholesome. Now this one would be born near Christmas. She opened the oak chest near the hearth and pulled out a tiny blanket of lamb's wool. She held it to her cheek, then folded it and rocked it in the crook of her arm. "Bye, baby bunting," she crooned softly. The babe within her kicked vigorously. "You will

9

live," she told the child. "You'll be a lusty son, I know it," she said. "And then we shall be a complete family, you and Derick and I—and what more could a woman ask in the whole of this world?"

Suddenly the polished trestle table began to glow, and then the entire room brightened. Rose stood up, laughing at herself.

"Sunshine! I had almost forgotten what it looks like." She went outside and lifted her face toward the sun, letting it draw out all the oppressive cold that the constant rain had brought. She had come out without her cap, and the sunshine made golden glints in her light brown hair.

"Catch those sunbeams in a jar, and we will have them for the next rainy day," Derick called to her. He was standing outside the smithy, his dark, handsome face flushed from the heat of the forge.

Wedded four years and my heart still catches at the sight of him, thought Rose. She lifted up her skirts and walked over to him, carefully avoiding the puddles. The sun, coming out in strength now, drew steam from the stone fence which divided their garden from Widow Terrel's. An insistent wind swept the crumbled clouds across the sky.

"Dearling, do you think they will return?" Rose asked as she watched the departing clouds.

"Shield God!" exclaimed Derick. "I've mended the last hoe that was hidden in the farthest corner of the smithy. If the weather stays not fair and farmers do not bring their oxen to be shod, we'll not eat."

Rose clasped his hand and looked up into his gray-green eyes. " 'Tis market day in Saffron Walden and we do need to buy a cradle—" she began.

"And please will I take you to market?" Derick finished. "In truth, Rose Haler, you are more interested in a fair pretty than a cradle." He laughed and held her to him. "If it wasn't for that swelling, you'd look like a child whining for a Bartholomew baby."

Rose flounced off toward the cottage. "Never you mind, Master Haler," she called over her shoulder, "I'll just stay inside my clammy cottage and rot away."

"Nay, fetch your cap and cape, Mistress Sauce, and we'll away to Saffron Walden.—Ned," he called to his hammerman inside the smithy, "finish up that cold work and bank the fire. Mistress Haler and I are off to market."

By the time they arrived in Saffron Walden, both Derick and Rose were spattered with mud. Derick had carried his wife over many water-filled wagon ruts, so he paused to catch his breath when they reached the edge of the Common. Rose tugged at his sleeve.

"Let us not tarry here. I want to see everything," she said.

"Aha! I wist you had more in mind than a cradle," Derick said as he let her pull him toward the market. Neither of them had ever mentioned the first cradle, the one Derick had fashioned himself for their first child. After the child had been born dead, Derick had removed it from the cottage while she was asleep. Only since this child had quickened within her could Rose make plans for its birth.

It seemed to Rose that all of Saffron Walden was out on the grassy Common. Stalls had been set up along the bordering row of elms. Baskets, cheeses, linens, pies—all sorts of household goods and foods were displayed. Horses and oxen were tethered awaiting inspection. Except for a few children playing in the wet grass, most of the townsfolk seemed to be gathered at the far end of the Common. As Derick and Rose moved toward the crowd, they saw that the townsfolk were forming a circle around an open spot of ground where a stake was being set into the ground.

"A burning. A witch is to be burned!" exclaimed Rose. "Oh, Derick, let's go home."

"Not a witch," said a dirty-faced boy about twelve years old. " 'Tis a heretic they're going to fry."

Two men were unloading bundles of faggots from a wagon, and the crowd pressed closer to the stake, pushing Rose, Derick and the boy along with them.

"And you cannot leave," the lad warned. "Here come the sheriff and his officers. He's ordered all of Saffron Walden to watch."

"But we're from Boxton," said Derick as he tried to steer Rose away from the spectators.

"Ah, then you'd not be knowing the heretic," said the boy, who had attached himself to them like barnacle. "He's a pewterer from over in Maidstone, but he was born here. John Newman's his name."

Derick stopped in his tracks. "Newman? I do know him. Rose, I've drunk ale with him many a time at the White Horse. John Newman, a heretic?"

The sheriff rode up on the opposite side of the crowd, and above the murmur of the crowd he shouted orders to his officers.

"He's just a little banty cock on a big horse," whispered one of the townsmen beside Rose.

"Spanish cap on his head," said another scornfully. "He daren't wear it in London, sheriff or no, or the 'prentices would set upon him with trudgeons. The Queen's Spanish consort and all his like are hated there."

"I had it from a peddler," said a beldame leaning on her staff, "that the Spaniard was leaving Her Majesty and sailing back to Spain. Good riddance, I say." She spat on the gound. "She should have married an Englishman. 'Tis God's judgment on her that Queen Mary's barren."

Rose winced at the mention of the Queen's barrenness. *Monarch she may be, but a woman still,* thought Rose. *And a woman was born to mother. At least I have a constant husband and another child in my womb.* "Derick, we must go," she said aloud. "The sight could mar the child in me."

Before he could reply, a loud murmur arose from the crowd as the prisioner was led to the stake. Once again Derick and Rose were pushed forward with the spectators, and directly behind them stood one of the sheriff's men with a club in his hand. There was no leaving now.

A hush fell over the crowd as Newman removed all of his clothing except for the white shirt which hung down to his knees. In spite of herself, Rose looked at the condemned man through a gap in the ring of people before her. She had never seen a heretic before. She knew, of course, that heretics had to be killed. Heretics and witches not only blasphemed, but also led the souls of commonfolk straight into hell. She watched Newman bow his head for a moment and then step up to the stake. The sheriff's men began binding him to it with chains.

This man doesn't look evil. He looks—she strained to see his face—*Mother of Mercy, the set of his jaw and the lock of black hair falling across his forehead—he looks a brother to Derick!* She felt faint and leaned her head back on Derick's chest.

He put his hands on her shoulders to steady her. "Close your eyes," he whispered in her ear. " 'Twill soon be over. It is the Newman I know," he said aloud, "but why?"

Rose tried to keep her eyes shut, but the suspense of waiting for the fire to be lit was even greater when she couldn't see what was happening. Besides, she could not shut out the sounds of the crowd.

"I'll vow it takes over-long to roast him in this damp weather," a man in a moth-eaten gray cloak called out.

"If them faggots are as green as they look, 'twill take to sundown," replied another man, as he lifted his child up for a better view.

Rose finally opened her eyes and watched as the officers placed bundles of faggots at Newman's feet and then piled them around him until the faggots reached as high as his chest. A priest mounted the makeshift pulpit, and while he unrolled a sheaf of paper, one of the officers lit a torch. Everyone was silent as the priest cleared his throat and began to read.

"John Newman, late of Maidstone:

Because you have despised the Holy Mass, calling it idolatrous and wicked,

Because you denied the right of priests to give absolution for sins, claiming it is against the Word of God,

Because you have preached these treasonous and false doctrines in the counties of Essex and Kent.

You are condemned as a heretic and sentenced to die by fire."

The priest lowered the document and looked at Newman. "If you recant now, mayhap God will spare your soul from the eternal fires of hell. How say you? Will you recant?"

Everyone waited expectantly for the condemned man's reply. John Newman's lips began moving but he could not be heard. His eyes were lifted up toward the sun. He was praying.

"Put fire to him!" shouted the sheriff. The officer with the torch lit the bottom layer of faggots. The crowd pressed forward. Suddenly, a young man broke from the ring of spectators and ran up to the stake. He attempted to tie around Newman's neck a leather thong on which hung a cloth bag.

"What's that?" asked a woman.

"Bag of gunpowder," answered the boy beside Derick. "Flames take hold of that and—whoosh, it will be over."

An officer grabbed the young man and shoved him into the crowd before he could tie on the gunpowder.

"You'll not rob us of a good show," he threatened the young man with his club. "Stay back or there'll be a roasting for you!"

The fire began to take hold of the wood at Newman's feet and a gentle breeze fanned the flames. A woman cried out, "Lord Jesus, receive your martyr with loving arms today!"

"Amen," said a voice behind Rose.

The flames began to lick at Newman's feet. Rose realized with horror that unless the uppermost bundles of faggots caught fire quickly, the poor man would suffer for a long time. As if to echo her thoughts, the woman prayed aloud again.

"God, God, let the fire burn fast!"

The wind rose and set loose reeds swirling around the small clearing. The highest faggots caught fire and soon Newman was overcome with the thick, black smoke. The prisoner gasped, gulping for air, then fell forward, his body straining against the chain at his waist. His head dropped toward the flames. The black forelock caught fire first, then the rest of his hair quickly blazed. The stench of burning hair and flesh blew toward Rose. The ground whirled under her feet and the sounds of the crowd became a roar in her ears. Then she blacked out. When she awoke she was lying under a tree on the road back to Boxton, her head in Derick's lap.

"I'm to blame," he was saying, stroking her forehead with his calloused fingers. "I should have known what was up. All the news of the county passes through the smithy. Travelers waiting for their horses to be shod, peddlers carrying more gossip than wares — something about the warmth of the forge must loosen men's tongues. Someone must have mentioned that Newman was to be burned today. I turn 'em off in my head while I work, the wagging tongues." She sat up and he helped her to her feet. "Forgive me?"

"Ah, dearling," she said as they began the walk home, "I've become a weakling to let one man's death upset me so. I've seen men killed before. When I was a young thing in London, a day wouldn't pass but what you could see a bloated, murdered body floating in the Thames, or a beggar full of sores dying in the street. One day Papa took me to St. Bartholomew's Fair, outside the London Wall in Smithfield. My brother Robin had cried to go along with us, but he had been naughty and Mama wouldn't let him. I'm sure Papa didn't know that an execution was to take place that day. Papa was a gentle man and took no pleasure in other folk's suffering. Mama, though, would have loved to see it. Often she would tell me about Anne Boleyn's execution. Why, she even knew how many strokes of the sword it had taken to sever the head from the body. Mama felt a sort of kinship to Anne Boleyn because I was born on the same day as Anne's daughter, the Princess Elizabeth."

Derick lifted her over another mud puddle. "Then why were you not named Elizabeth?" he asked.

"Because Papa said I was his little London Rose."

"And now you are Boxton's fairest bloom," he said with a laugh. "And with mud all over your stems."

"But to my story — and don't turn me off as you do the gossips. At the fair, while Papa was bartering at another bookseller's stall, I slipped away and ran over to a large gathering of people. I crawled through the forest of legs right up to the front, just in time to see an executioner disembowel a man. The poor victim must have been screaming, but I don't remember hearing a sound. I just recall seeing his mouth — opened wide with his lips curled back over his teeth." She shuddered.

"I didn't cry or faint then. It was as if I were looking at pieces of a puzzle. My brain couldn't put what I saw into shape. Papa found me then and carried me away. He let me sleep with Mama and him that night in case I had nightmares, but I had none. The man meant nothing to me. In my little world, the only people that mattered were Papa and Robin and Mama."

They stopped on a small hillock just above Boxton. "But what happened today was different. John Newman wasn't a high-born traitor. He was a craftsman from a neighboring village, a man like you. Oh, Derick, he even had your appearance." She buried her face in her hands and began crying.

"There, there, my whiting," said Derick as he patted her awkwardly on the shoulder, " 'Twas not me. Just a man of old acquaintance. Why, I wist I have not spoken to him in five years' time. Poor fool, trying to make sense out of religion. I marvel at him. Why did he do it? Why let them lead him to the flames over the mass? He had a head on his shoulders, Newman did—or used to. Why all the bother over the Church?"

"Ah well," he said as they came to the door of their cottage. "How about a bit of bread and some porridge after we scrape the muck from our shoes? And God's oath, look at us! We've come back without a cradle."

Rose shivered as she entered the houseroom and began laying a fire. *"No cradle,"* she whispered to herself. *"Oh, St. Elizabeth, may this not be an evil omen."*

Chapter Two

ROSE SNUGGLED down in the flock bed and let a warm, delicious sleep ebb and flow over her. In the middle of the night she had finally found a comfortable position and now she was loath to move from it. She wished she could remain in this cozy, drowsy state until she awoke one morning to find she had been delivered of a lusty man-child. *Dream on, slug-a-bed,* she drowsily told herself.

Suddenly she opened her eyes. Something was wrong. Had there been a knock on the door or a voice calling? She rolled over. Derick was gone from his place beside her, but there were still impressions in the mattress from his huge shoulders. She awkwardly sat up. *It's too light. He's let me oversleep again. What might the neighbors think if they knew I was still abed?* From the time Derick had courted her on her aunt's prosperous farm and then had brought her to Boxton as his wife, some of the housewives in the village were ever quick to find fault in her. Her gowns were a bit too fine for her station; the slight upturning of the corners of her mouth was mistaken for a snobbish smile. Even though she had been orphaned as a young girl and had been taken to live on the farm outside of Boxton, she was still known by a peevish few as "that woman from London." "What makes them green with envy, I know well," she had once told Derick. "I've caught the best man in Boxton."

"Marry, 'tis true," Derick had replied, ever undermodest. "And what's more, the gossips are envious because you can read."

He had always been proud that she could read. Derick had gone to work with his father in the smithy when he was just a small lad and had never learned to read or write.

'Tis the reading that lost me sleep last night, she thought as she hurriedly dressed and coiled her long hair into a knot at the nape of

her neck. In the two months' time since the burning of John Newman, Derick had become marvelously curious to hear the Scripture. Last night again he had asked her to bring out the Great Bible which she kept hidden under her linens in the bedchamber chest. Even though it was now forbidden for commoners to own a copy of the Scriptures, she had cherished the Holy Book because it was the only inheritance she had from her father.

"Read to me about the bread and wine," Derick had requested last night. It had taken her a long time to find the spot in the Gospel of St. Matthew, chapter twenty-six:

" 'And as they were eating, Jesus took bread, and blessed it and brake it, and gave it to the disciples and said, Take, eat; this is my body. And he took the cup, and gave thanks, and gave it to them saying, Drink ye all of it; for this is my blood of the new testament, which is shed for many for the remission of sins.' "[1]

She had read it to him several times slowly as he repeated the words after her. He then asked her to read the part where the Lord said, "I am the door," but she couldn't find it and yawned so much that he had told her to put away the Book and go to bed. She had kissed the back of his neck and told him to hurry to bed and keep her warm, but she had fallen asleep while he yet sat by the fire.

This morning the sweet, dusty smell of autumn wafted into the cottage and with it the sound of a hammer hitting iron. "Derick. He must be starving!" exclaimed Rose. He wouldn't get his own bread to break his fast, not even if his belly growled like a pit-bull. He had lived alone in the cottage for several years after his father had died. During that time he had stubbornly refused help from kindly housewives and had muddled along doing his own mending and cooking. Since he had gotten him a wife, however, he would go without rather than do a woman's work.

Rose dipped out a mug of cider from the keg in the corner of the houseroom and wrapped a slice of maslin bread around a wedge of cheese. As she went out of the cottage with Derick's breakfast, she saw the cooper's wife carrying a clothes basket down toward the river. "Double drot," Rose muttered. "Washday. I'm late for washday. More fuel for the gossips." As she walked around to the front of the smithy, she recognized Sheriff Pike's big roan tied up at the post.

"Too fine a horse for such a mean little man," Derick had told her after the first time he had shod the horse. Derick admired good horseflesh, but he approached strange horses with caution. He had

---

[1]Matthew 26:26-28

good reason. The kick of a skittish horse had left a jagged scar from his temple along the jawline. His close-cropped beard concealed most of the scar, but the memory of the injury kept him careful during each shoeing.

As she approached the entrance, Rose heard loud voices over the hammering. The sheriff, in his Spanish cap, another man, and a boy were standing just inside the smithy with their backs to her. Derick was at the anvil and Ned, the hammerman, was working the leather bellows at the hearth.

"Are you threatening me, blacksmith?" the sheriff was shouting.

"I wist not that I had threatened, sir." Derick's hammer punctuated his words with heavy clangs and sent sparks flying from the red-hot metal on the anvil. "I but said that if I attempted to do such work for you now"—he hit the metal again—"with my arm so tired, this hammer might fly out of my hand and strike someone." Derick's face was glowing from heat and anger, and beads of sweat had gathered on his beard. In the semi-darkness of the smithy, he looked to Rose like an angry bear, reared and ready to charge.

The sheriff stepped back, almost colliding with Rose but yet not seeing her. "Your helper, then," he said, "he can forge the chains for this heretic's legs." He gestured toward the boy.

Derick kept working and didn't look up as he replied, "Nay, sir, he cannot. My hammerman is not skilled to do such work."

During the tense silence that followed, Rose brushed past the three men into the smithy. "Husband, here is your breakfast—oh, pardon me, gentlesirs," she said, forcing herself to curtsy to the sheriff and his officer. She stared at their captive. He was a lad of about fourteen and wore the blue smock of an apprentice. There was a large bruise on his forehead, and his lips were cracked and swollen. His hands were bound with a rope which the officer held as if he were leading an ox.

Pike doffed his hat to Rose. Seen at a distance, Rose had thought the sheriff had a handsome face, but now up close his features looked as if they were carved from a cake of tallow. His eyes were dull, like the eyes of a mackerel's which had lain too long on the fishmonger's cart. In spite of the heat from the forge, Rose felt a chill pass through her.

While the sheriff was eyeing Rose, Derick motioned to Ned to give the boy a drink. Ned took a dipper of water from the barrel by the forge and put it to the boy's lips.

"Meddler!" The sheriff knocked the dipper out of Ned's hand. "This whelp is on his way to the stake. All the water in the Thames won't quench his thirst there." He motioned to the officer to take the boy outside. Pike shook himself slightly. "If I had the time, blacksmith, I'd teach you a thing or two about obeying your betters." The two men mounted their horses, and the lad struggled to stay on his feet as he was pulled down High Street behind them.

Derick slammed his hammer down upon the workbench, took off his leather apron and went outside with Rose. He sat down under the shade of the great oak and drained the mug of cider in one gulp. "God's oath, the little pippenjay," he swore.

"So young a lad," said Rose. "Did you see the look in his eyes!"

"Aye, as scared as a trapped hare—and just about as dangerous. Leg irons," he snorted. "The lad wouldn't have been able to walk." Derick attacked the bread and cheese. "Do you know what his crime is?" he asked between mouthfuls. "They say the lad was caught reading the parish Bible. He told the priest he wanted to find out for himself what the Scriptures say. For that he'll have his life snuffed out before he reaches manhood. Such a dangerous criminal."

Rose was used to seeing Derick angry, for he had a spleenful nature, but the sheriff had stopped just short of arresting him a few minutes before, and his anger made her very uneasy.

"I think it not right to harm a mere child for reading the Scriptures, dearling," she began, "but do you not think it dangerous for men to go against the wisdom of the Church, to disobey its learned leaders?" Even as she spoke she made a mental note to bury her father's Great Bible in the garden. *No use to court disaster,* she thought.

"Wisdom? Bah!" he said scornfully. "Look you, Rose, religion is all in the whims of whoever wears the crown. When I was a lad of eight, they had an English Bible in every parish church, because that was how King Henry wanted it. I remember well that the cooper's father would read it aloud for all who cared to hear, sometimes even when the mass was being said. It made the priest fair blow his top. Then about four years later the King decreed that commoners, housewives and servants were forbidden to read the Scriptures."

Rose remembered that time. She had been living on the farm then and had assured her aunt that she had destroyed her father's Bible; she had actually hidden it in an old straw beehive in a storeroom in the barn.

Derick's voice brought her back to the present. "Then in '47 Henry dies, and who wears the crown?" He sounded so like a schoolmaster that Rose could barely keep from smiling.

"The boy King Edward, Henry's son," she answered.

"Aye, and then everyone was allowed to read the Holy Book again, and 'tis said they even said mass in English in London. The commonfolk tolerated it, except for a few old biddies who cried for the old ways. Then, two years ago—"

"Edward died and his sister Mary came to power," she finished for him.

"And she brought all the popish ways back. Smudging our foreheads with ashes on Ash Wednesday, creeping to the cross on Good Friday. 'Tis as if the monarchs were singing a children's rhyme. 'We put the feast days in, we take the Latin out, we give the altar a shake, shake, shake, and turn it all about.' And we're supposed to go, humble as you please, wherever they pipe us, even to the mouth of hell."

Rose stared at Derick in amazement. "Why, dearling, I've never heard such impassioned speech from your lips, not even when you asked me to be your wedded wife!"

He gave an embarrassed laugh as if he had surprised himself. "Ah, well, I reckon I never gave religion much thought until I watched John Newman die for his beliefs. I still understand little of it." He stood up. "There were two men at the White Horse yesterday when I stopped in for a mug of ale before supper. They talked about God in a way I—" he stopped and shook his head, laughing. "High conversation for a blacksmith," he said as he helped her up. "Back to the forge where I belong."

Chapter Three

MOST OF THE WOMEN of the village were already at the riverbank when Rose arrived. This would be the last washday before winter and all the housewives had brought large bundles of soiled clothes. Three women were stirring clothes in cauldrons of boiling water. Others were spreading their clean clothes to dry upon bushes that grew along the riverbank, or hanging up linens on ropes strung between trees. Mattie, the miller's oldest daughter, had a birch switch in her hand and was herding a group of children away from the river and the busy women.

"Rose, is that you?" Cecily Packingham called. She was kneeling at the river's edge, dipping her soiled clothes into the water and slapping them with a paddle. "I thought your time had come—I was about to go to your cottage." Cecily's eyes were wide and unfocused as she watched Rose approach.

Poor, dear Cecily, thought Rose. She was very nearsighted but refused to squint. She smiled at everyone and everything and apologized to doors, trees and sleeping dogs as she stumbled through life. Although tall and big-boned, her vacant gaze softened her appearance. It had been a joke in the village that only a half-blind girl would have married Christofer Packingham. The innkeeper had a large, bulbous nose that drew all attention away from his friendly grin. Derick and Chris had been friends since childhood; Rose, the outsider, and Cecily with her affliction, took to each other immediately.

Rose knelt beside Cecily. "Derick let me oversleep again," she said as she dipped his Sabbath shirt into the river and rubbed it gently between her hands. "He's afraid I'll lose this child. He wants a son so badly."

"Christofer was snoring loudly when I left the bed," said Cecily.

"Two travelers dawdled over their cups last night. I finally went up to the bedchamber; Chris let them sleep on the tables because the rooms were taken. I saw Derick talking to them late yesterday afternoon. Are they friends of his?"

"Nay," said Rose, "they talked of religion and their conversation just struck his fancy, I suppose."

Cecily put her hand on her friend's shoulder. "He'd best beware. The strangers tried to engage Chris and me in a religious debate later in the evening." She lowered her voice. " 'Why,' one asked, 'should the Bishop of Rome be telling Englishmen how to worship?' The other called the mass 'Jack in the Box!' You well know Chris, he brushed them off with a joke, saying his brain was too ale-pickled for serious talk. But, Rose, they have treasonous ideas."

Rose frowned. "Are the two strangers still at the White Horse?" she asked.

"Nay, they set off at dawn," Cecily replied.

"Good. Then Derick will forget about them," she said as she picked up her paddle and gave his nightshirt a strong slap.

Half an hour later they stopped to rest. Rose sat up and rubbed her back. "Look, Cecily, there's Alice." Cecily stared blankly toward High Street. "No," said Rose, "over there, by the cauldrons." She pointed to a middle-aged woman in a nun's habit who was struggling to carry a large basket full of clothes.

"The Widow Terrel has servants to do the wash. She shouldn't make her own sister do it," said Cecily.

"The Widow takes pleasure in offering charity and then making Alice work like a servant because of it. Some people have that way about them. Their favors are put upon a helpless soul as chains until she's bound up in them."

"Not my Chris," said Cecily. "His charity flows as freely as cider from a broken keg. The filthiest beggar or crone that whines for a cup of ale gets it from him unless I happen by."

"But that's a different kind of charity. Alice is the Widow's own flesh and blood. When the Queen dissolved the marriages of all former religious, Alice had to give up her marriage to Barnabe. Since there were no more convents, she had nowhere to stay and was forced to live with her sister. I happen to know that Barnabe Coates pays the Widow dearly for his former wife's keep."

"The 'Widow' this, the 'Widow' that—why do we not call her by her Christian name?" asked Cecily as she returned to her washing.

"What is it, then?" asked Rose.

Cecily laughed, "I know not. Since she has the finest home and the sharpest tongue in the village, I wist that no one has ever been friends with her long enough to find out."

Rose took a stick and idly drew a heart in the muddy riverbank. "Poor Barnabe," she said. "He sorely misses his Alice. Can you imagine being married for years and then being told that you could not live with your husband anymore, that you could only speak to him at church or market—and then only in the presence of witnesses?"

"I would not mind for a time," said Cecily. " 'Twould be a joy to be free from keeping his clothes clean." She held up Chris's huge nightshirt.

"I couldn't live without my Derick across from me at table, beside me in the bed," Rose said softly. She drew another heart entwined in the first. "Cecily, look at those bird tracks. That's Robin's sign."

"Robin's?" Cecily peered at the tracks in the mud. "They look more like the tracks of a plover."

"I meant my brother, Robin," Rose replied. "When we were small we made up secret signs. Mine was this." She drew a rosebud. "Robin's was a bird track. Once Mama beat him for carving his sign in a table."

"Why did not your aunt bring your brother from London, too, when your parents died?"

"He was old enough to be apprenticed out so my aunt apprenticed him to a printer, a mean man that my father had despised. I never knew his name, but I remember when the man came to take Robin away. I was not even allowed to kiss my brother good-bye."

"Did he not write to you?" asked Cecily. "Or come down from London?"

"Nay," said Rose. "When I first was taken to my aunt's farm, I cried every night for Robin and imagined that he would come and rescue me like a knight of old, but he never came. My aunt made several journeys to London, but she would never take me along or allow me to send a message to Robin. 'Bury the past,' she would say. 'He has his life and you have yours.' But I think she was afraid she would have to provide for him if we kept in contact." She sighed. "I pine less for him now that I have Derick, but now and then my heart longs to see my brother."

"Well, at least your aunt brought *you* from London. And I am so glad she did," said Cecily.

"Are you housewives chatting or washing clothes?" said Alice as she came toward them. She was breathing hard as she set her basket down and slowly knelt by Cecily to rinse her laundry in the river. "As I joined the biddies at the cauldrons they were twitting about the both of you thinking yourselves too high and mighty to wash with the rest of them—but I gave them a look that curled their toes, I wager."

"Gossips, all of them," Rose said with fervor.

"Ah, 'twas the same at the convent," said Alice. "Gossip was the sin most confessed, I ween, and least repented of." She gave a little moan and shifted her ample body into a more comfortable position as she wrung her clothes out.

"Knees bothering you again?" asked Cecily.

"Aye," said Alice. "The years of kneeling on cold stone morning and night have caught up with me."

"Were you happy as a nun?" asked Rose.

"In my fashion, I was content within the walls, but when all the nuns were turned out and I came here and met Barnabe, I found there was room in my heart to love both God and a husband." She sighed. "And now, even though they've made me don these black robes again, I still love my Barnabe."

Alice brushed a tear from her eye and Cecily shifted the conversation. "Rose was telling me of her brother she left in London. London! Imagine living but a two-day journey from the city and never seeing it—not that I could see much—but the fairs, the Bridge—"

"I would that I could worship in St. Paul's," said Alice. "And you, Rose—would you like to go back?"

"Aye, to find my brother, someday, but 'twould be a hard task. There was not a clue among my aunt's things as to what his master's name was or where he lived."

"Look yonder," said Alice, pointing to a woman a hundred yards downriver. "There's a clue that Mistress Martin has quarreled with her husband again. She's beating his shirt until the color runs from it. Wishes he were in it." She sighed and held up a cloth. "Alas, if this were only Barnabe's shirt instead of my sister's kirtle."

Cecily stood up. "If I do not spread these things out to dry, I shall still be laundering come Sabbath."

"And I," said Rose. She picked up her basket of wet wash and then dropped it, doubling over in pain.

"Fetch Derick!" Alice ordered Cecily. "Here, my girl," she said gently as she helped Rose to sit down on the grass. "Since the time of Mother Eve, the curse of childbearing has been its pain, but think on the joy that comes later. There's a good girl, rest your head on old Alice. I'll see you through it. Many's the healthy babe I've brought into this world of woe."

Despite Alice's soothing words, fear gripped Rose, contracting with the pain. *What if the child is turned the wrong way or the cord is wrapped about its neck? It's all too sudden—I'm not ready—*A second strong contraction blocked thought from her mind, and she was conscious only of the wave of pain rising, rising, gripping until it was almost unbearable. The agony crested, ebbed away; but before relief came the next wave of pain shut out all consciousness.

Rose could barely recall being lifted up in Derick's strong arms. She could not at all remember being carried home, but here she was in her own bed. Now the pain, constant, gripping, brought her to the surface of consciousness, and a deep moan rose from her dry throat.

"Push, Rose—in the name of heaven, push!"

Rose bore down so hard she felt the blood pounding in the top of her head. The pain! Every vein throbbed with it; every muscle tensed against it; every nerve resisted it! The pain engulfed her, red and pulsing, tearing at her flesh—

Then—ah!—the pain was gone, so suddenly it startled her. It was over! Her child, her precious, longed-for child, was born! Rose let go and drifted into an exhausted sleep, lulled by the murmur of voices near the foot of the bed.

It was dark. The pain had given way to a blessed blackness—cool, isolated darkness, and release. Far away, in the distant recesses of that darkness, Rose heard vague sounds. They rose and fell in the familiar cadence of speech, but she could not make out the pattern of the words. She fought her way toward the light of full consciousness, straining toward the meaning of the voices.

The Widow's nasal voice was first to pierce the dark dream. "Give it up, Alice. 'Tis dead, just as the one before." Rose kept her eyes closed tightly, concentrating on the words. "Silly fool, my sister," the Widow muttered close by Rose's ear. "Just because she wears a nun's habit, she thinks she can raise the dead."

Red, thought Rose, fighting the stupor of sleep. *Yes, red. All babes are red—red and wrinkled, not fair and perfect as the mother's eye sees. Yes, red, like all newborns. And such a good baby—not crying, nor demanding its first meal; silent, sleeping, allowing its mother her rest after the hard birthing.* "Think of the joy that comes later," Alice had said. *The joy—yes, the joy of Derick's child. Such a good babe!*

"Please," pleaded Cecily in a whisper, "you'll awaken Rose. Let her get her rest before she faces the news."

The news, thought Rose, *the precious news of my baby—our baby, Derick's and mine.* Rose kept her eyes still shut as the two women straightened her bedclothes.

"Poor little thing, poor dear." Alice's voice drifted in from the houseroom. "Never opened its eyes upon this wicked world."

"'Tis their own fault, both of them," the Widow whispered loudly. "Too lusty at love. I have seen them in their garden of an evening. Acted as if they were courting, they did. He cannot stand beside her without touching her. 'Tis unseemly for a man and wife to behave so. God is punishing them by denying them the fruit of their lusts."

"Nay, sister," Alice retorted, returning to the bedchamber, "if God denies children to loving couples, then it follows that the Lord would have blessed you and your departed husband with a hundred children!"

"Hold your tongue with me, Sister Sauce. What know you of a *real* marriage? You wed that idiot cobbler when you were past your prime and fresh out of the nunnery. Indeed, as soon as the convent was dissolved and you were given permission to marry, you fairly jumped into the marriage bed with your cobbler. And now that our Queen has the piety to undo such fleshly unions, you moon about after your 'dear Barnabe' like a hound in heat."

"Enough!" Cecily demanded. "Widow, you are thanked for your help, but we can manage now," she insisted. "Alice will fetch the priest and I will go and tell Derick." The cottage door closed quietly behind the three women.

Behind Rose's still-shut eyes the pain returned—not sharp and gripping this time, but throbbing dully, numbly—the pain of sorrow. Rose turned on her side and buried her face in the coverlet. *Dead! God in heaven, how can it be? Once more brought to the threshold of motherhood, only to be turned away. The swaddling clothes—the 'broidered caps—why? Babies die, and toddling infants—Cecily lost her own little girl to the coughing sickness last wintertide, but not before she had the memory of holding her, of feeling the wet little mouth against her breast. Why am I denied? God in heaven, why? WHY?*

Had she screamed aloud? She did not know. The pain beat in her eardrums, deafening, insistent. Would it never cease? God, would it never, never cease?

Rose heard the cottage door open and close and the sound of heavy boots upon the rushes in the houseroom. The footsteps paused. *He must be looking at the baby,* she thought.

"Derick?" she called

"Aye, dearling," his voice was muffled.

"Is it—is it a girl-child?"

"Nay," his voice broke, "a son."

Rose pushed herself up to a sitting position. Her heart felt so heavy she could barely breathe as she forced out the words, "Bring him—to—me."

Derick started to say something, and then walked slowly into the bedchamber. He was carrying the small linen-wrapped form in his hands, not cradling it as a woman would, but held out in front of him, as a king might carry a golden coffer containing all his treasure. He lay the baby on the coverlet and knelt down by the bedside, watching as Rose lifted up a fold of the cloth and stroked the baby's still damp hair.

"Black hair, and lots of it," she said softly. "He would have looked the image of you." She held the baby to her breast and rocked him, humming a lullaby.

"Rose, no," Derick stood up quickly and turned away. She could see his shoulders heaving as he sobbed.

"Oh, forgive me, forgive me, I've failed you again!" she cried out.

He rushed back to her side and held her and the baby close to him. "Nay, dearling. You could never fail me. 'Twas just the sight of you singing to—him." He took the child from her and laid him gently at the foot of the bed. He sat beside Rose and she pressed her head on his shoulder. "We're young," he said. "We'll yet have a living child, but—" he looked at his little son lying so still upon the coverlet—"I marvel how God could make such a perfect little body and not—and not give it a heart that beats." Their tears mingled as they embraced.

At last Rose pulled away and said the thing that had been gnawing at her mind. "Do I love you too much, Derick? The Widow says God is punishing us because we love each other too much."

"That prune-faced bag of wind!" He slammed his fist down upon the bedpost. "She doesn't know the reasons of God. Who does? Who can fathom His courses?" He paused and looked down at the chest which contained the Great Bible. "There's some that say, though, that it's all in the Book if we but read it for ourselves."

"Oh, no, the Bible—" Rose said frantically." 'Tis dangerous— we must bury it—those men—keep away—the burnings—" She tried to get out of bed.

"Stay, Rose." Gently, Derick pushed her back against the pillow and covered her up. "There, there, sleep now. No more talk of danger. Rest, now, rest. I will take our babe and wait in the houseroom for the priest. Close your eyes, there, my fair Rose. Sleep."

Chapter Four

AS WINTER approached, Rose regained her strength, yet she remained withdrawn and unresponsive to Derick's attempts to cheer her. He had even fashioned a little bird of ornamental iron to perch upon the bedpost. After weeks of gloomy evenings spent with a silent wife, Derick began visiting the White Horse for a cup of cheer after dinner. By Christmas Rose had finally put aside her grief, but she had a new worry. Derick would often leave his work early and tramp through the snow to the inns and alehouses of neighboring villages.

The first Sabbath morning of the new year, Rose slammed the cottage door behind her, wrapped her cloak about her and walked toward the church. The crisp air cooled her burning face but not her anger.

"He comes home late at night, will not get up and go to mass, and thinks a kiss will mend it all." Her breath came out in little puffs of moisture as she walked down High Street talking to herself. "He knows he could get fined or even thrown into prison if he doesn't attend service. He cares not, the slug-a-bed."

She had awakened at dawn and had spitefully thrown the coverlet off Derick as she got out of bed. He had merely rolled over, smiled and pulled her back into bed with him. She usually welcomed his early morning embraces. When he was half-asleep he was even more gentle and loving than usual. This morning, however, she had pushed him away. "Not on the Sabbath," she had said primly.

"But you were asleep when I came home," he said. He reached for her again but she stood up. She had not really been asleep when he came in last night, but she had lain motionless, her back to him as he undressed. He had not been singing or staggering about as he did

28

when he had too much to drink. No, he was sober when he came home last night, and now as she thought of it, it worried her even more. At first she had thought his frequent visits to inns and alehouses was his way of getting over his grief. When their first child was born dead, he had buried himself in his work. If he chose to bury himself in his cups this time, she could see no real harm. But he was not drinking that much—wenching, then? *Nay,* she shook the thought from her head. *Still, why does he go to other villages to do his drinking? Because Cecily would know if he carried on with another woman at the White Horse?*

She reached the path that led to the church. It was early and there was no sign of any other worshipers. She hesitated. She wanted to be inside kneeling in prayer before anyone had a chance to ask why Derick wasn't there, but first there was something she must do. She broke two sprigs of holly from one of the bushes that lined the stone wall beside the church and went around to the graves.

The gravestones were covered with a fine frost, and they gleamed in the weak sunlight. When they were newly wed, Derick had brought her here to show her the graves of his parents, his grandparents, and his great-grandparents. There was a lovely continuity about the village churchyard that appealed to her. She knew not where her own parents were buried in London. Perhaps, since they died of some terrible fever, their bodies had been burned. She little thought when first she visited this final resting place for the people of Boxton that she would lay her own babies to rest here.

She stooped beside the two unmarked graves. As she brushed dead leaves from the frozen mounds of earth, the strong longing to hold a baby, to brush its silky cheek with her lips again began to overtake her. With a sigh, she placed a sprig of holly on each grave. "Sleep, my little babes," she whispered softly, then rose hurriedly and retreated to the safety of the sanctuary.

As she entered the church, Rose found the air inside the sanctuary damp with smoke from burning candles hanging low over the pews. She genuflected, then knelt to pray. When she raised her head she saw that two people were now sitting several rows in front of her. Alice and Barnabe Coates. Here, at least, they could talk together. Alice was sitting bolt upright; from behind, the heavy folds of her black wool habit made her look like a fat black bear. Barnabe was bent forward, his shoulders stooped from years bent over his last. They sat apart but were talking in low tones to each other. Rose had little sympathy for their plight this morning. *They may have to be apart physically,* she thought, *but at least there is no secret wedged between them.*

As the villagers began filling up the pews, Rose looked straight ahead and tried to keep her eyes off the statue of St. George to the left of the sacristy. St. George had been her favorite statue when Aunt Katheryn had brought her here to worship. It had been a handsome statue then. With his muscles bulging beneath his armor and his great sword in hand, St. George had looked capable of slaying the largest of dragons. Rose had dreamed of marrying a man as strong as the saint, someone who would protect her against all foes. Little wonder that when Derick had come to the farm to shoe the horses, she had fallen in love with him at first sight.

But a few years ago when the young King Edward was still on the throne, a man, either drunk or full of Protestant zeal, had lobbed off the tip of the statue's nose. The mutilation had given St. George a battle-scarred look as if he had clashed swords with the devil himself. (Many statues of saints had been mutilated during the brief time when the Protestant king and his Protector were ruling.) Later, a sculptor had been commissioned to restore the church statuary, for now St. George sported a new white plaster nose on his smoke-stained face and looked more like a mummer in a play than a militant saint.

A noisy crowd now filled the church. The priest entered and the celebration of mass began. There were whispers and laughter and coughing all during the ritual, but when the priest finally raised the host and said, "Hoc est corpus meum—" a man called out, "Lift it higher, we can't see in the back!" Most villagers believed that seeing the pyx which held the Holy Bread would ward off illness.

"Shut you up, Jack Willis. You are still too drunk to see anything, you malt-worm," his wife retorted. There followed a loud discussion by some housewives as to whose husband drank the most ale. The priest, accustomed to such raucous outbursts, went on with the ceremony.

Rose shut her eyes tightly and prayed, "St. Elizabeth, hear my prayer. God gave you a son when you were past the time of child-bearing. Ask the Blessed Lord to give me one while Derick and I are still in our prime. Heal our marriage. Take away whatever has come between us, whatever is causing him to act so strangely. He is my life, dear St. Elizabeth. He is all I have to love."

When Rose arrived home, Derick was standing outside the cottage waiting for her. All the way home she had resolved to be pleasant and forgiving to him, but at the sight of him, resentment welled up in her, and she thrust her chin out and tightened her lips as she approached him.

"Looks more rain than snow we'll be getting today," he said as she brushed past him into the cottage. She took off her cloak and added a log to the fire.

"I'll boil some salt cod and reheat the pottage," she said, not looking at him.

"I'm not hungry," he said. He stood in the doorway, rubbing his hand across the lintel. "Why did you rush out this morning? I wanted to talk with you."

She banged two wooden trenchers down upon the table and flung a spoon beside each. "And I wanted to keep you out of trouble! No one spoke to me, but surely the hawk-eyed Widow Terrel and others noticed your absence from service." She took a loaf from the ambry and began slicing it.

"Last night you lay in bed like a stone—" he began.

"And last night you left me alone again while you went carousing. 'Tis freezing. Come in or out, but shut the door." She turned her back on him and began stirring the pottage. She swallowed to keep down the knot in her throat.

"I go not carousing. I've wanted to tell you, to divide what's been given—" he paused and waited for her to respond, but she ignored him. "There's a place I must visit. Mayhap your anger will be cooled when I return. We'll talk more then." He closed the door gently behind him.

Rose waited until he was outside and then threw the spoon down and flounced down on the bench. "Where would he be going on a Sabbath afternoon?" she asked herself. Travel between villages was not allowed on the Sabbath. Curiosity got the best of her and she moved the kettle off the fire, grabbed her cloak, and followed him. Stopping by the corner of the smithy, she peered around it just in time to see Derick turn down the lane leading north from the village. It was a sunken lane, winding through the countryside. Most of the trees that formed the hedgerows on either side of the lane were barren of leaves, except for an occasional holly. Rose waited until Derick turned a bend in the lane and then followed.

The sky was darkening and an icy wind nudged her along. *A fool's journey,* she thought, *tracking my own husband as if I were a highwayman about to steal his purse. But something is stealing our married joy, and I'll not wait for him to tell me about it. Whatever, whoever it is, I'll see it for myself.*

She continued trailing him on the winding lane for about a mile. Turning a bend, she saw a long stretch of lane ahead. Derick was not in sight. *He must be running,* she thought, *and if he is, I'll never catch up.* She stopped beside a stile to rest a moment. She noticed faint footprints on the path that led over it to the Saunders' Farm. *He could not have gone there,* she thought. Old Saunders lived alone with just two house servants. There were a few herdsmen and their families which lived in outlying cottages, but she could hardly imagine any reason for Derick to visit them. He had taken neither tools for shoeing a horse nor physic for doctoring an ox. Besides, he would not risk death by working on the Sabbath.

She climbed over the stile and followed the path through a field to the farm buildings. The sky was almost black now with thick rainclouds. The main path ran around the outbuildings and directly to the farmhouse, but there was a newly trampled path leading straight to the back entrance of the barn. Although her hand trembled as she reached for the latch, overwhelming curiosity forced her to open the door. She slipped into the barn and waited as her eyes became accustomed to darkness. She smelled smoke but saw no rush lights or candles lit.

"Mama, I'm frightened!" a child cried out.

"Who's there? Who—who are you?" Rose asked in a quavering voice. A hand touched her shoulder and she gasped and ran outside. Someone caught her arm and spun her around.

"Oh—Derick—it's you. I was beside myself with fright—"

"Softly, Rose," he cautioned.

"But why are you here?" she whispered. "Who is inside?"

He pulled her back until the side of the barn hid them from view of anyone in the farmhouse. He scowled at her. "You should not have come. Too dangerous. I said I would talk of it later."

Her heart was beating wildly, but she thrust her chin out, folded her arms and stood her ground. "Derick Haler, by all that's holy, you *will* tell me—now!"

He studied her for a moment and then sighed, "As you wish it. Come inside, then."

There was the sound of rustling of straw as they entered the barn, and Derick closed the door behind them, this time taking care to bolt it. "Fear not, friends, this is my own wife," Derick called out into the darkness.

"You said nothing about bringing your wife, Haler," a man's voice said accusingly.

"She might be a spy," a woman's voice said.

"I'll vouch for Mistress Haler. Never would she harm a soul." Rose recognized the voice of Agnes, who had once been her aunt's maidservant and now kept house for old Saunders.

"Will you swear to keep quiet about who you see and what you hear in this place?" asked a man's voice close to Rose.

"I will," she answered, "but—"

"Sit you down with the others," the voice said with authority.

Rush lights were lit and now Rose could make out about fifteen people in the barn, all of them, except for one tall man, seated on straw in a semi-circle. She recognized the wheelwright, his wife and their little daughter. John, the wheelwright's apprentice, was there also. The rest of the people, most dressed in servants' apparel, were strangers to her. *They must be from outlying farms,* she thought.

Except for Agnes, they all watched her warily as she and Derick sat down beside the wheelwright's family. The tall man, obviously in charge, stood before the group. *He's a Londoner, for certain,* thought Rose, *and here for what purpose, to stir another uprising against the Queen as Wyatt did? But why would Derick mix up in rebellion? He would never fight to put Princess Elizabeth on the throne.*

The Londoner cleared his throat, then said, "Brothers and Sisters, let us pray."

Mother of Mercy! thought Rose. *So that's it—heretics! Another kind of rebel—and just as dangerous.* The blood was pounding in her head as she heard the man's "Amen."

"Before I begin the sermon," the man went on, "I have some sad news. Samuel from Pine Farm has been taken. One of his neighbors informed on him." There were murmurs of dismay in the group, and one of the women began crying softly. "This must be our last meeting here," he continued. "If they have Samuel, it is only a matter of time until they try to apprehend the rest of us."

Agnes twisted her apron with her gnarled hands as she said, "Pastor Barcock, I thought nought of it at the time, but two days ago I saw my master talking to the sheriff." She looked around at the group. "Oh, but I'm certain he knows nothing about our meetings. Why, Master Saunders sleeps so soundly on Sabbath afternoons that I must needs awaken him with a cowbell."

"Let one of the sheriff's men try to take me and I'd cripple him for life," said the young apprentice, jabbing at the straw with a pitchfork.

"Nay, John," replied the pastor, "our Lord commanded us to love our enemies."

"But, sir," the boy retorted, "do you think the Lord wants us to run to the fire? What of the wealthy believers who have fled to the Continent? Do you think it fair for poor folk such as us to have to endure persecution while they are safe?"

The minister shuffled the pages of the Bible before he answered. "Of a truth, it is hard for mortals to fathom God's designs, but good is coming from our brethren's exile. They have taken many young men with them and are training them for the ministry toward that glad day when popery is abolished from our land. They are printing pamphlets against the wicked Queen and that Romish wolf, the Archbishop. Besides, I believe that if we can escape death without denying Christ, we should do so. You, John, for instance, could easily hide in the woods if danger threatened."

The wheelwright spoke up. "My goodwife has family in the North. If worse comes to worse, we could flee to them, but whatever comes, God is on His throne."

"Whether we live or die, we can but speak the truth," quoted an old woman, her voice quavering with emotion.

"Amen," echoed the congregation.

Rose sat numbly as the minister read the Scripture and preached a long sermon. She kept her eyes on the barn door, expecting the sheriff's officers to burst in any moment. Everyone else—including Derick, to her dismay—gave the minister his complete attention, seeming to drink in everything he said and responding with "amen" and " 'tis so." Even the wheelwright's little girl had relaxed and fallen asleep in her mother's arms. At last, the minister closed the Bible and asked, "Is there any other word before we dismiss? Yes, Sister?"

A middle-aged woman who had been sitting alone at the back of the group stood up. She was holding a bundle which she carefully unwrapped. "These are my husband's boots," she said quietly. "As you know, he was burned in Smithfield a fortnight ago. I want one of the brethren to have his boots. They are finely—" she started sobbing, and one of the women went to her and put her arms about her.

"But Mistress Robbins," Pastor Barcock gently protested, "you could sell the boots to buy food for you and the children. I know your house has been taken from you."

Mistress Robbins lifted her tear-stained face. "Nay, sir, neighbors have taken us in, and I spin for our food. I have sold his tools and will cut down his clothes for our oldest son, but he was so proud of his boots. I want someone of the faith to have them."

"Thank you, dear sister," the pastor said as he wiped a tear from his own eye. "I'll see that they go to a worthy brother." Then he addressed the group, "I go up to London tomorrow. I shall take what I can to help the poor believers in prison. The wretched souls in Newgate Prison are deprived of every comfort. Does anyone have an offering with which I can buy bread for them? John, pass your cap around."

Everyone contributed. Derick pulled out his purse and emptied all the coins in it into the cap. *He gives it all away,* thought Rose, *and how shall we buy flour for bread? With prayers?* Then she felt ashamed of herself. *Poor misguided creatures. 'Tis a horrible fate for anyone to lie in a foulsome prison, whatever the reason.*

"Now we shall sing a psalm if the way is clear," the pastor was saying. "Jason?" Rose just now noticed the young boy up in the hay-loft. He must have been there all the time, keeping watch.

"All clear, sir," the boy answered and the group began singing softly, "The Lord is my shepherd; therefore can I lack nothing—"

After the psalm, the congregation dispersed, each family taking a different route to their home.

When Rose and Derick arrived at the cottage they argued at length. With tears and pleadings she told him that it was pure folly to attend heretical meetings, especially since he admitted to her that he was not certain in his mind that he could accept their beliefs.

"Calm yourself, dearling," he said at last; "you have my word that I will not attend. Not now. Still, something in their teaching draws me. The more I hear the Lord's own words spoken from the Book—Rose," Derick turned to face her, "He spoke plainly so that a fisherman or blacksmith could understand."

Rose had begun clearing the table, making undue noise.

" 'Tis clear your ears are closed on the matter," he said. "I'll not offend you with it then." He walked outside into the light rain that had begun falling.

Chapter Five

"DON'T HURT ME," the little boy pleaded. He held his hands tightly over his left eye.

"Now, now, lad, I'll not hurt you," said Derick. He picked the boy up and set him on the workbench near the forge. "Sit here 'til I've finished with this bar of iron," he told him. He began pumping the bellows until the coals glowed. The little boy flinched as the heat in the smithy increased, but he took his hands away from his eye and watched with fascination as Derick pulled the bar of iron from the coals. The tip of the bar glowed bright cherry red.

"Thank you, Master Haler," the child's mother said. "I told Nicholas that the smith was the only one who could cure his stye."

"Just leave him here for an hour or so and he'll be quit of it," said Derick as he began working at the anvil.

"Good-day, then," said the woman, "and good-day to you, Rose."

Rose had come in to get the last of the winter's smoked meat, which hung from the rafter in the smithy, and had stayed to observe Derick with the boy. *In spite of his great strength,* she thought, *my man's as gentle with children as a woolly lamb.* She watched Derick at the anvil. With the tongs in his left hand, he held the red-hot iron on the anvil, and with a small hammer in his right he tapped the spot on the bar where he wished Ned to strike with a larger hammer. The rhythm of their work and the heat from the forge soothed her. She smiled to see little Nicholas leaning forward as he watched the men from his perch. His face was beet red from the heat. The lad didn't realize that this was a blacksmith's "cure" for styes. Just his sitting so close to the forge allowed the heat to eventually open the stye.

All the glow I feel inside cannot be blamed on the forge, thought

Rose with a blush. The night before she and Derick had partaken of the joys of wedlock, not of necessity, but as one heart and soul. *A far cry from the wooden embraces he has given me of late,* she thought. Although two months had passed since her discovery of the secret meeting, and, as far as she knew, he had not consorted with the heretics, still he had seemed a different man to her, a man with a worrisome problem. Last night, however, he had come in from work and had scooped her up in his arms, acting as free of care as a wandering minstrel. He had let her oversleep this morning, and now she planned to prepare a special love feast for his midday meal.

"I'm off to market now," she told him, smiling coyly. "I'll be making your favorite food today, fresh oatcakes—with raisins."

She waited for a look of pleasure on his face. Raisins were such an extravagance, she could never bring herself to buy them except for an important occasion. Derick didn't even look up as he said, "Good, take your time at market. Stop and visit Cecily if you wish. I've a lot of work to finish before I stop for a meal."

"But, master, you said—" began Ned.

"Never mind what I said," Derick replied abruptly. "Let's finish this bar before it cools." Rose huffed out without a word.

After she had put the salt meat in a pan of water to seethe, Rose set off to market. *Let him eat day-old bread instead, for all I care. Master Hot and Cold!* She deliberately tarried long at the market. *I'll be so late in fixing his food that he will ache with hunger,* she thought. It was a difficult task, for Boxton market was a sorry affair compared to Saffron Walden's. Besides, since it was early March, the farmers had not much to offer but cheeses, a few old apples and dried corn. She was so sick of winter fare. Spying some packets of raisins, she hesitated and then bought one. "Not for him, for me," she told herself. But he did so love the raisin oatcakes, and he was so loving last night—and everyone needs a treat now and then. She decided to hurry home after all and start her cooking. She walked past a group of women who were gathered around a peddler.

"Rose, wait," Cecily called.

"Oh, I didn't see you," Rose said as she turned around.

Cecily came up laughing. "Oh—ho, and who's the blind one now?" She took Rose aside and whispered, "I've just heard the strangest news. Lizbeth, you know, the wife of the wheelwright—she's disappeared. The entire family is gone! Anna's husband went to their place to pick up a mended wagon wheel this morning. There was no sound from the cottage, 'though he knocked and called loudly. Thinking the whole family might be abed with a fever, he and

Chris broke in. Not only was the family gone, but also the cooking pots, food and clothing. But that's just the half of it," she said as she squinted over her shoulder to look for eavesdroppers. "There was talk last night at the inn. Sheriff Pike has vowed to root out every heretic in the county. Not for piety's sake, I ween. He wants the Queen to hear of his great loyalty and to grant him some of the lands taken from the heretics."

Rose tried to act unmoved by the news and barely caught the packet which had slipped from her grasp. "What—what has that to do with the wheelwright?" she asked in a trembling voice.

"Why, you were at mass last Sabbath. Did you not see? I was beside them. When the procession passed, Lizbeth and her husband turned their back on the parson. They've fled, lock, stock and barrel, because the sheriff was going to arrest them. Rose, they are *heretics*!" She peered at her friend. "Why, Rose, dear, you look as if you'd seen a ghost. Don't take it so to heart. We didn't know them well, none of us—Well!" She watched the blurred image of Rose hurry down the lane toward the smithy. "I little thought a bit of gossip would upset her so."

As she walked, Rose argued with herself. *Derick's in no danger; he's attended mass with me almost every Sabbath these two months. But what if he's conversed with dangerous men again? And what if the wheelwright is captured and betrays him? Nay, he would not. But Sheriff Pike hates Derick so . . .*

She ran into the smithy, but the only one there was old Ned, asleep in the corner. She heard the voices of Derick and another man coming from the cottage, and she burst in and found Derick and William, the cooper, seated at the table. The cooper was writing on a sheet of foolscap.

"Oh, back so soon?" Derick looked up guiltily. "Could you leave us for yet a little while? We'll be soon finished."

Rose tossed her purchases down on the table, almost upsetting the ink well, and flounced out. She started down the lane, back toward the center of Boxton.

"Rose, come back," Derick called as he ran after her. Several women coming back from market stared at him as he ran past and caught his wife by the arm. "William says we need your signature on the paper," he said. Fuming, but overcome with curiosity, she allowed him to lead her back into the cottage.

William held out the quill to her. "Here, Mistress Haler," he said as he pointed to a spot on the foolscap, "right below Derick's mark. You can write your name?"

"That, she can," said Derick proudly, "and read. She can read anything."

Rose put the pen down. "Then first let me read what I'll be signing."

Derick banged his fist upon the table. "Never you mind. I am your husband and I order you to sign!"

She grabbed the pen, jabbed it into the ink well and scrawled her name at the place William had indicated. Then she ran into the bedchamber, slamming the door behind her. She heard the murmur of voices and the outer door closing.

When Derick came into the bedchamber a few minutes later she looked up from the bed. " 'Tis your will I witnessed. You've heard of the wheelwright's leaving, and you think he'll inform on you and the sheriff will arrest you."

"Nay, not a will—and I've no fear of what the wheelwright might say. I just thought it wise to deed over the cottage to you, along with the smithy and the land. You own it outright now."

"But why?" she insisted.

"Oh, these are troubled times," he said lightly, "and a man likes to know his wife would be taken care of if anything happened to him."

"You've fallen in with the heretics again," she accused. "I knew it." Her eyes betrayed her confusion. "But last night you seemed so lightened of a burden that I thought you at last had put all that away from your mind."

"Lightened of a burden," he repeated with a grin. "Aye, 'tis so." As he sat down beside her, he continued eagerly, "I did speak with the wheelwright yesterday and—" he searched for the right words. "It was my birthday, dearling. I've been born again."

Rose looked into his eyes, as alight as a child's at Christmastide. "Those are the same words the heretic preacher spoke," she said slowly.

"I wish I knew all the words to tell you how real God is to me now," he said.

"You've said enough. Oh, Derick, the danger!"

He looked down at his hands. "I have counted the cost. That is why I have deeded everything to you. The Crown can confiscate a believer's property—but it will be safe in your name."

"But you'll not be taken if no one knows."

He held her to him. "Remember when you tried to hide your feelings for me when first I courted you?" He laughed. "Still, it bloomed in your cheeks and shined in your eyes. What if someone had asked you outright then, 'Do you love that blacksmith, Derick Haler?' Could you have denied it?"

"Nay," she said softly, and kissed him on the cheek. "I was bursting to talk of you with anyone who would listen." She snuggled against his shoulder. "Tell me, then, of this new love for God."

He stood up and began pacing the floor. "First of all, I came to see—" he raised his voice in his excitement, "that God is not in rite and ritual." A gust of wind blew through the wind-eye. Rose thought she heard a creaking in the houseroom.

The shutters, she thought, but didn't interrupt Derick when he was pouring his heart out to her.

"Take the mass, for instance," he continued. "It is an evil and idolatrous ritual. God doesn't live in that piece of bread, He—"

She motioned him to be silent. She had seen a shadow fall across the doorway. "Who's there?" she called, praying it was only Ned.

Widow Terrel peeked in and said in a simpering voice, "Oh, pardon me, I didn't mean to intrude."

"I heard no knock," said Derick as he brushed past her into the houseroom. Rose followed him and noticed that the cottage door was ajar.

"The door was open and you seemed to be so busy that I thought I would just set these down on the table and leave," replied the Widow. She held out a jar to Rose. "My famous pickled quinces." Her eyes were gleaming, and she looked to Rose like a hawk who has spotted a tasty morsel to shred with its sharp claws.

Rose forced herself to take the quinces from the Widow and to thank her. She waited until she saw the Widow enter her own cottage, and then said worriedly to Derick, "She heard every word, I know she did."

"I think not," replied Derick. "She could not have been inside long enough. At most, she'll trumpet it about the village that we've had another quarrel. That should make her happy," he said grimly.

"She's never liked me, nor you," said Rose.

"Ha! There was a time she took quite a fancy to me," he said, putting his hands on Rose's shoulders.

"When? You never told me," she said. She leaned back against his chest and relaxed a little.

" 'Twas passing strange. Six years ago, soon after her husband died, and I was living here alone, my own father having died the year before, she—well, she set her cap for me."

"Oh, no," Rose giggled.

"Aye," said Derick, warming to his subject. "I was such a green lad, I thought at first she was just being neighborly. She invited me to sup with her several times, and she mended my cloak and often brought me food. One evening, after I'd stayed long at the White Horse, I came in here to find a dinner spread out on the table and sounds coming from the bedchamber. I grabbed the poker from the hearth and pushed open the bedchamber door, expecting to find a thief. There she stood in a nightgown, with flowers in her hair, her arms extended to me. I took one look at her, turned, and ran for my life. I slept out in the fields, and the next morning when I returned home there was no trace of her. Not even a crumb from the fine dinner she had spread out." He laughed and said, "So you see what a silly old woman she is. We've naught to fear from her."

Rose looked out the wind-eye toward the Widow's cottage. "Oh, no, dearling, you are wrong. Because of what you've just told me, I fear her. I fear her very much."

Chapter Six

"PLEASE DON'T LET them take him, please, oh, please, don't let them take him," Rose prayed silently over and over. Derick lay asleep beside her. She moved closer to him and felt the heat from his body and smelled the faint scent of iron that was always on him. He was her "man of iron," they had joked. He rolled toward her in his sleep, and she held his hand against her cheek. His knuckles were large and rough with scar tissue from countless scrapes and cuts. *My love, my only love, even in the dark I can rehearse your every feature. I thought I knew the mind of you and the heart of you as well. What emptiness was in you that this heretic religion filled? Is there yet some lack in our marriage? Oh, surely if I had borne a living manchild you would not be courting danger now!* She went over in her mind the events that had followed the Widow's eavesdropping.

The Widow's interruption had seemed to dampen Derick's zeal, and he spoke no more of his conversion. After he went back to the smithy that morning, Rose tried to busy herself cleaning, but she finally stood her broom in the corner and took off her apron. She had to find out for herself how much the Widow had heard. She emptied the quinces into a bowl, washed out the jar and carried it to the Widow's cottage.

Alice answered the door. "Why, Rose," Alice said with a puzzled look on her face. "Come in." Rose had never paid a call before. Alice led her into a handsome parlor and motioned for her to sit in one of the ornate chairs.

"My sister is not here, so we might as well visit in comfort," Alice said, settling her large body into a chair.

"Where did she go?" Rose blurted out.

Alice raised her eyebrows. "Why, to market, I suppose, but 'tis rather late for it. Did you wish to see her?"

Rose hesitated. Although Alice was bitter about her marriage being dissolved, she was faithful to the Church. She might not be sympathetic toward Derick and his heretical beliefs. "Your sister brought me some quinces," she finally replied. "I was returning her jar."

"Quinces?" Alice snorted. "Throw 'em out. No, don't do that—some poor dog might eat the stinking mess. Bury 'em. Our maidservant ate some yestermorn and had a horrible attack of the runs." She waited for Rose to laugh, but she was on the verge of tears.

"When she came over, she walked right in and she heard Derick and me—uh, quarreling," said Rose.

"Old Sharp Ears can hear a pin drop in the midst of a cattle sale."

"Alice, did she say anything to you about us?"

"Nay, all she asked me was if I'd seen the sheriff in the village when I took flowers to the church this morning."

"The sheriff? Oh, Mother of Mercy!" cried Rose.

"Now then," said Alice soothingly, "if quarreling with your husband were an offense, all the housewives in Boxton would be in the stocks. Rose, wait!" she called. But Rose was running out the door and toward the smithy.

Despite her pleadings, Rose could not convince Derick to escape. That evening he had eaten a hearty meal and had gone to sleep early while Rose sat in the houseroom, watching the dying fire and waiting to hear pounding on the door. At last she had gone to bed, and now she lay beside Derick chanting her prayer.

When she finally drifted restlessly to sleep, she dreamed fitfully. It was May Day, and a tall Maypole bedecked with flowers had been set up in the middle of the village green. Derick was leaning against the pole as the May Queen and the morris dancers skipped round and round him. Suddenly three milkmaids danced up to Derick and began pelting him with flowers from the beribboned buckets they carried. The flowers fell in a heap at his feet, and the blossoms burst into flames. Rose tried to reach him to pull him away from the flaming flowers, but she moved slowly, as if she were running through a river of honey. At last she reached him, but when she touched his arm, his whole body turned into ashes and crumpled to the ground. She screamed as all the revelers danced faster and faster around her.

She awoke with her mouth wide open in a soundless scream and her jaw aching. She clung to Derick's back and sobbed. He stirred in his sleep. As she drew in a shuddering breath, she thought she heard a scraping noise at the door. She sat up and strained her ears. Hearing nothing, she sighed and snuggled back down against Derick.

"Open in the name of the Crown!"

Rose screamed. Derick staggered out of bed and stood in his nightshirt, shaking the sleep away. "What's that?" he mumbled.

"'Tis the sheriff! Flee!" she cried. She jumped out of bed and gathered up his hose, boots and cloak. "Haste, you can go out the wind-eye and escape to the woods." Her hands were shaking as she handed Derick his clothes. The sheriff pounded on the door until the entire cottage seemed to vibrate with the sound. Derick dressed slowly and then embraced Rose.

"Away, away! They'll break the door down soon!" she urged, but he kissed her hair and took one long, last look at her.

"Stay in here 'til they've gone, dearling," he said as he went into the houseroom, closing the bedchamber door behind him. Rose threw the coverlet around her shoulders and quietly opened the bedchamber door just a crack in time to see Derick unbolt the outer door and three men rush in. The two officers quickly grabbed Derick's arms and tied his hands behind him. He did not resist. Rose knew he could have overcome the two of them easily and walked right over the sheriff to freedom if he had wished to.

The sheriff picked up a mug of last night's ale from the table, sniffed it, and splashed the ale in Derick's face. "Wake up, blacksmith, you seem to be dreaming. No struggle at all from you? Or do you need a hammer in your hand to make you bold? Haven't you had enough fire in your work?" He sat on the edge of the table knocking big clods of mud from his riding boots. "Your neighbor tells me you love flames so much you wish to bathe in them."

Derick looked him in the eye and said calmly, "If you mean the Widow Terrel, has our great High Sheriff nothing better to do than listen to a gossipmonger?"

Pike shook his whip in Derick's face and said shrilly, "You were heard by a respectable member of this village to say that you believed the mass was 'evil and idolatrous,' and you said the Host was but a piece of bread. Do you deny this?"

Rose held her breath as she waited for Derick's answer. *Tell him you were misquoted, tell him anything but the truth,* Rose pleaded silently. *They have no proof but the word of a known troublemaker.*

At last Derick spoke. "Nay, I'll not deny it, for I but spoke the truth and will speak it again."

"My thanks to you, blacksmith," said Pike, "for you have sealed your own fate with those words. If I had my way we would dispose of you now rather than take you to London to be questioned. Bring him along," he ordered his officers. "We'll find a cozy place to keep him until morning."

As she heard Derick's confession, Rose froze with fear and leaned against the wall. Finally she willed herself to get dressed and staggered into the houseroom as the door burst open. Alice charged inside and bolted the door behind her. She was wearing her woolen nightdress, and her sparse grey hair stuck out in wisps. She grabbed Rose in a bear hug.

"Forgive me, forgive my parents for spawning a creature like my sister! I didn't know, I swear I didn't know. I heard her in the parlor a while ago, cackling with glee. She was watching out the wind-eye when the sheriff came to your cottage. She even boasted it was her doing." She released Rose and paced back and forth. "May she fry in hell!"

Rose fought off the paralyzing fear that seemed to seep through her body. "Don't give way to despair," she told herself. "Do something!" Then turning to Alice she asked, "Where think you he'll be lodged tonight?"

"I was hidden by the hedge when they brought Derick out," said Alice. "One said the shed behind the church would make a fitting gaol. I'll stay with you through this evil night. I dare not be near my sister or I might commit a mortal sin and kill her." She wrinkled her wide brow and said gently, "You must know, Rose, that if Derick truly has become a heretic, he's in danger of losing his mortal soul."

" 'Tis his life I fear for now," Rose cried as she began bustling about the room. "Here, fetch me that sack," she said as she gathered up some cheese, a loaf of maslin and the packet of raisins. "He never had his oatcakes," she whispered to herself. She lifted her skirts and began tying the bread knife to her leg with some twine.

"Dear girl, have you gone mad?" Alice cried. "You cannot hope to free him yourself."

"I must do something." Now that she had begun moving, a great surge of energy made her feel strong enough to do battle with giants. She started for the door.

"I'll go with you," said Alice.

"In your nightdress?" Rose smiled. "You're a true and loyal friend, Alice. Abide here—and pray."

It was a clear moonlit night. Rose shivered and pulled her cloak about her. "Now what, my brave housewife?" she asked herself. *Chris*, she thought. *The innkeeper is a true friend of Derick's, but I wist not that he knows of Derick's taking up with heretics. 'Tis not as if I could say, "Derick has been captured by cutthroats." I've no doubt then he would grab a stout club and rush to his defence. But if Chris dared to interfere with the law, he could lose his license and his livelihood, and few the men that would risk that for another's religion. The priest? He surely knows Derick is no threat to Christendom. But he's new to the village, and he cares little for any of us. 'Tis I, I alone who must do it,* she grimly decided.

As she approached the church, she strained her eyes to look for any sentinel hidden in the ribbons of shadow cast by the elms along the path. She took a deep breath and went toward the shed behind the church.

"Halt. Who goes there?" One of the sheriff's officers had been sitting on a keg in front of the shed, and now he barred her way with his staff.

"Mistress Haler," she answered in a high frightened voice. "Please let me see my husband. I've brought food for him. See?" she held the open sack toward him. He jerked it out of her hand.

"Thanks to you, Mistress. My belly was gnawing."

"But my husband—I must see him," she said frantically. *If she could but cut his bonds with the knife she had concealed,* she reasoned, *he could easily overpower the lone guard and escape into the woods.*

"Nay," he answered, "the sheriff vowed it would be my neck if I let anyone come near the smith until he returns." He tore off a chunk of bread from the sack with his teeth.

"At least let me go to the door and speak with him," she pleaded. *Somehow I can shove the knife under the door,* she thought.

" 'Twould do no good," mumbled the guard as he chewed, "I've put him to sleep with this." He waved his staff. "Now—home with you."

Rose made as if she were leaving but went round instead to the South Porch of the church. She slumped down on a cold stone bench to wait for the dawn. She was not used to taking things into her own hands, and the encounter with the guard had crumpled her boldness. Derick had always decided things for the both of them. Oh, how she would argue and fuss if he didn't agree with her, but there was comfort in not having to make a final choice. *Now in this life-and-death situation, I am no use at all,* she thought. *If I could but talk to Derick, he could tell me what to do.*

She fell down on her knees and tried to pray, but the words wouldn't come. *After all,* she thought with welling resentment, *God allowed him to be arrested despite my prayers. Why should I think He will answer them now?* She looked down at her hands, washed white by moonlight filtering through the carved stone lattice. "What helpless things you are, either for prayer or combat," she whispered. Derick had sorrowed whenever he saw her hands scratched from stripping rushes or reddened from washing clothes. He would kiss her palms and say, "Would I were the lord of a manor; then your hands would know no harder task than 'broidering a cloth."

"Oh, Derick, my dear, dear love!" she cried. "What's to become of you? Will you ever kiss these hands again?"

Sometime during the night she fell asleep with her head against the bench. At dawn she awoke to the sound of horses' hooves and pressed herself into the corner of the porch. Through the lattice she could see Sheriff Pike riding up with several other men. One of them was pulling a rope to which six manacled prisoners were tied. There were four men and two women, and they all looked as if they, too, had been roused from their beds. One of the men was still in his nightshirt and neither of the women wore a cap. They were all splattered with mud and struggling to keep their balance as they were pulled along. Rose waited until the procession had gone around the church, and then quietly followed them until they stopped in front of the shed. The older of the women fell and the younger tried to help her up.

"Have mercy, give my mother some water and food," begged the young woman.

One of the officers spoke up. "Sir, if we don't give them a bit to eat and drink, some of them, especially the women, won't last on the journey to London."

The sheriff dismounted and stroked his horse's muzzle. "Very well. Give them something, but mind you, don't fill them full. This is no pleasure stroll. The Bishop wants them free from comfort. A little misery will make them recant and save them from burning, he says." He laughed. "I know better." He turned to the captives. "You fanatics want to die—'tis part of your queer religion. So be it. I'll be joyed to assist you in the matter. Each time I rid the county of another of your kind, 'tis a feather in my cap."

As the officer gave the prisoners each a sip of water from a jug and placed a bit of bread in their bound hands, Rose crept closer toward the group. Several villagers had come near to see what was taking place and she stood by them. One prisoner, an old man with bits of leaves and twigs in his long beard, kept muttering, "I did no wrong," and looked hopefully into the faces of the bystanders. Another, a ruddy youth, glared defiantly at the guard. A third, a mere child, had the same frightened look that she had seen on the captive 'prentice in the smithy.

She took in the tragic scene only superficially, for her main thought was of Derick.

"Ho, keeper, bring out the other fish for my string," the sheriff called. Derick was led out of the storehouse. His arms were still bound behind him and he had a cut on his forehead that was matted with dried blood and straw. He blinked his eyes and swayed a little as he was brought out into the sunlight. Rose ran to him and embraced him before anyone could stop her.

"Dearling, away!" Derick cried urgently. Rose turned to the sheriff.

"Please, sir, release him—he's done no harm."

The sheriff looked her over slowly. "What a pretty little beggar you make, Mistress Haler. If you miss your husband's company so soon, we have room on our little fishing line for you." He touched her cheek with his riding whip.

"Let her be!" Derick shouted and lunged at the sheriff, but the guard grabbed his shirt and threw him off balance so that Derick merely grazed Pike's arm with his massive shoulder as he fell to the ground. One of the officers knocked him insensible with a club. Another pinioned Rose's arms and kept her from going to Derick.

"How touching," said the sheriff as he pulled on his riding gloves. "Escort Mistress Haler back to her cottage," he ordered the one who held her. "And you," he said to the guard, "pour some water on the blacksmith and tie him up with the rest. We must be on our way."

When Rose entered the cottage, she found Alice asleep at the table and snoring loudly. Just as she was covering Alice with her cloak, Chris charged in with Cecily close behind him.

"We've just heard," said Cecily. She put her arm around Rose. "Why did you not tell us?"

"By my bones, I'd have broken the guard in two with my bare hands!" Chris bellowed. His face was red with rage.

"I knew not what to do," said Rose. "Oh, 'tis my fault, all mine," she sobbed. "If I had not been so ill-tempered, if I had let him speak of his new faith sooner, the Widow would not have heard—"

"He's been taken to London, then?" asked Alice as she rubbed the sleep from her eyes.

"Aye," said Rose, "and I must hasten to follow." She started for the door but Chris blocked her way.

" 'Twould do no good for you to follow after," he told her sooth-ingly. "Derick would go mad from worry if he knew of such a silly plan. The authorities have no real reason to detain Derick in Lon-don," Chris pointed out. "There's just the hearsay evidence of the Widow, is that not so?"

Rose shook her head. "The sheriff asked him straight out if he had called the mass idolatrous and Derick would not deny it."

Alice gasped. "Still—still, he has not been caught preaching these heretic thoughts in public. Surely the Bishop in London will just reprimand him and release him."

"Of a truth," said Cecily. "In a week's time, Derick will come walking in that door."

Chapter Seven

BUT A WEEK PASSED, and then another, and Rose had no news of Derick. She was alternately depressed and feverishly active during the long wait. One day she would lie in bed and stare at the ceiling; the next, she would scour her cooking pots, scrub clothes and give conflicting orders to Ned.

During the third week she was taken with a terrible nausea. At first she blamed it on her fears but finally recognized it for what it was—a sign that she was with child again. "What mocking fate is this," she wondered, "that a child was conceived on that happy night before Derick's arrest?"

Chris and Barnabe decided to go to London and seek word of Derick. Rose hastily wrote a letter to Derick hoping that if he were in a prison, a cell mate might read it to him. In the letter she told him she was well and loved him very much, and then, as a postscript, told him of her pregnancy. "Mayhap, the thought of a child to be born will cause him to recant of this nonsense," she reasoned.

The two men were discouraged and loathe to tell Rose of their findings when they returned. "He's not—they haven't—?" she cried.

"Nay, nay, 'tis not that, at least," said Barnabe.

"He's in Newgate Prison, a vile place, and has not yet been questioned by the Consistory. We gave the gaoler money to buy Derick food, but I'll wager he put it in his own purse."

"Here's your letter back," said Barnabe. "The gaoler would not take it in to him or bring us any word from him without a bribe, far more than we had."

The two men left and Cecily sat with Rose to keep her company.

"If they had planned to do him greater harm, they would have done the deed by now," said Cecily, trying to reassure her.

"I don't know what to think," said Rose. "I turn it in my mind, day and night. How could this happen to us? We're but simple folk, Derick was a blacksmith, nothing more or less. But the day we saw the burning in Saffron Walden was an evil day, I ween. From that time on, he sought answers to questions that were better left unasked."

"Men sometimes grow restless, and, well, a little addlebrained," said Cecily. "I heard tell of a thatcher who climbed down from a roof one day and disappeared. He was seen a year later selling oysters in Colchester!"

" 'Tis not the strangeness of Derick's actions that troubles me as much as the fact that he stands alone in his beliefs," said Rose. "Since the day we were wed we truly were as one, except for this. I try, Cecily, I try, but for the life of me I cannot see why he should disagree with what the Church has ordained. Can you?"

"I'm not the best to ask," said Cecily. "Attending mass is my lawful duty, so I do it and forget it as every Christian should," she admitted wryly.

Three more weeks passed. Alice offered to move in with her but Rose gently declined. She kept to herself more and more and took to wandering around the countryside from morning until dusk to exhaust herself. It was, she told Cecily, the only way she could assure herself of sleep at night.

Except for Chris, Cecily, Barnabe and Alice, the villagers kept well away from her. Cecily told her that Derick's capture was the main topic of conversation among the patrons of the White Horse. There, with tongues loosened by ale, villagers and farmers alike expressed both their amazement at Derick's sudden conversion and their common dislike of the sheriff. But face to face with her, they would merely nod to Rose and hurry by. Ned reported only disgruntled remarks by those needing shoes for their horses or mending for their tools. Work fell away quickly because Ned was not trained in all the smithing. Sadly, Rose decided to send Ned away to seek temporary work in Saffron Walden. He begged to stay, but she could ill afford to feed him with no income.

On the Sabbath morning of the sixth week since Derick's capture, Rose lay abed at midmorning. "I will not go to mass," she said aloud. "Why should I go to praise you, God? You let them take him. I hate you, I hate you!" she cried. "Oh, sorry I am, my God. I meant it not. Let him live, let him live," she cried into her pillow.

There was a light tapping on the door. She lay still, hoping the visitor would go away, but the tapping continued. She sighed and went to answer. *Probably Ned, asking to stay,* she thought. *The poor old man must not have found any work.* She would let him stay, of course, and would divide what little food she had left.

"Good Sabbath, Mistress Haler." The caller was a middle-aged woman with a basket in her hand. She smiled nervously as Rose stared at her. "Do you not remember me?" she asked.

"The Saunders' Farm—" Rose began; "you were there." She took a step backward and began closing the door. "You gave away your husband's boots."

"Please, wait," the woman said as she put her hand on the door. "I came to give you this"—she held up the basket which was filled with food—"and to pray with you. I have suffered what you are suffering now."

"Nay," said Rose as she pushed the basket away. "My husband will not die as yours did."

"It saddens me to tell you this," said the woman, "but my brother had word that six men from Essex will be brought from London prisons this week. They are to be executed in their own villages. I came to help you prepare—"

"I won't listen. Be gone!" Rose pushed the woman out of the way, slamming the door and bolting it. Then she leaned against it, trembling.

"I'll pray for you, dear, for both of you," the woman called out. Rose could hear her footsteps as she slowly walked away.

The following Friday she looked down from Miller's Hill at the winding road below which disappeared among the sloping fields on its way to London. On this, the highest point in Boxton, she could see smoke rising from several other villages nestled among the low Essex hills. The wind swirled her skirts as she gazed steadily toward London. This was the fifth morning she had kept her vigil on the hill. Several women hoeing in the nearest field below looked up at her curiously. When she passed the miller and his young helper as they opened the mill, the younger man had tapped his forehead and laughed.

They all think I've gone mad. Mayhap I have. But I feel that if I don't keep a constant watch, I'll never see his dear face again. He'll be set free, I know he will. What does that heretic woman or her brother know? The mill creaked as the wind slowly turned its wooden blades. Rose called softly in time with the creaking, "Come home, come home, come home."

"Rose." She turned to see Chris climbing the path toward her. He still had his apron on and his face was flushed from the exertion of the climb. In the distance she could see Cecily struggling to catch up. Rose ran to meet him.

"Derick?" she asked. "He can't have come, for I've been watching all morning."

Chris leaned on one knee and looked down at the ground as he caught his breath.

"Tell me," she demanded, "for God's love, tell me!"

"He's being held at Lord Endley's. They brought him back under cover of night. Pike was afraid of an uprising among the villagers, or so a fellow from the manor told me."

"But they will release him?" As Chris hesitated Cecily caught up with them. Tears were streaming from her eyes.

"My poor, poor Rose," was all she could say.

Chris looked away as he finally answered, and the words came out haltingly. "Tomorrow—on the Green—he's to be burned."

Rose felt the blood drain from her face and fell forward. Chris caught her and gently laid her down on the path. Her thoughts swirled in her brain. Cecily was talking to her, but she couldn't understand the words. The awful spectacle of John Newman's death flashed in her mind, but now instead of Newman's face, she saw Derick's as he choked on the smoke and his upper body fell forward into the flames. In her mind the flames rose and swirled through her own body and burned her heart to ashes, leaving a black, empty place. Suddenly she felt cold and limp.

Somehow Chris and Cecily managed to get her down the hill and into her cottage. After they had given her some cider, she was able to speak. "Why? Why?" she asked in a weak whisper.

Chris looked down at his boots. "The Bishop himself signed the order. Jack learned from one of the officers that Derick had been kept in stocks all the while he was in Newgate. A few weeks in stocks would make most men agreeable to anything for the sake of freedom. Not him." His voice broke. "He went before the Bishop and stood firm in his answers. He would not deny that he had slandered the mass. His answers to the Consistory so infuriated the Bishop that he ordered Derick to be burned straightaway."

Rose began tidying her hair. "I must see him. I'll put on my Sabbath dress." She giggled hysterically. "He calls me his beauty when I wear it. He'll recant. I'll convince him, will I not?" She began to pace the floor. "He loves me. He has just been misled." She tugged at Cecily's sleeve. "Come, help me dress. Chris can take me up to the manor."

"Nay, Rose," Chris protested. "Jack says Derick is heavily

guarded. You know Lord Endley—heart of a snake. He would not allow you to see him. Endley and the sheriff should both be slithering on the ground. I would squash them—like this." He stamped his huge boot on the ground. "Jack said he'd try to get in to see Derick when he brought food to the guards, and if he does he'll be bringing us word about now. I'll go out to watch for him."

Soon Chris returned. "Jack says that Derick will be brought into the village at dawn. He convinced the guard that he should be kept at the White Horse until—things are ready. 'Tis good news. Mayhap once he is inside the inn, I can bribe the guard to let you see Derick."

"But did Jack see Derick?" Rose asked eagerly. "Did he bring any message for me?"

"Aye, he said to tell you that he loves you with all his heart and desires that you send him something for—for tomorrow."

"Well, what is it?"

Chris sighed and turned his head away as he answered. " 'Tis his wedding shirt he wants. Derick wishes to die in his wedding shirt."

Chapter Eight

AS THE HOURS passed, the horror of Derick's impending death had gradually given way to hopeless resignation. After Rose had cried on Cecily's shoulder until there were no more tears, she had insisted that her friend leave her to wait out the night alone. At dusk she had taken Derick's wedding shirt from the bedchamber chest and, having found a slight rip on the sleeve, had begun to mend it. Through the long night, however, she had carefully sewn over every stitch in the shirt several times. The thumb and middle finger of her right hand were bloodied from countless needle pricks, while her mother's silver thimble lay unused on the table.

Now, just before dawn, she was still sewing. The dying fire and the flickering light from a rush taper illumined the white shirt on her lap. In and out, in and out she jerked the needle through the yoke of the linen shirt. Her hair fell across her face as she bent over her work. At last she tied a knot, bit off the thread, and carefully folded the shirt. She had made this shirt for Derick and also her own wedding gown.

She thought back to her marriage day. After the ceremony, Cecily and some of the other women of the village had dressed her in her nightgown and carried her into this cottage. They had sprinkled sweetsmelling herbs on the bed and, with much giggling, tucked her into bed and placed two mugs of wine on the bedstand. One of the housewives had whispered instructions to her, but her head had been swimming with so much excitement that she had not listened. Whatever the marriage bed offered, she joyed to partake of it with Derick—and that was all that mattered.

She stared into the fire and remembered the ribald joking and scuffling as the young men had carried Derick into the bedchamber.

He had picked up the the poker from the hearth and chased them outside, then bolted the door and locked the shutters. They had beat on the door for a while and then left, singing a bawdy song. She remembered Derick as he stood at the foot of the bed, his face aglow with excitement and wine. He had smiled shyly at her as she folded down the coverlet.

"So long ago," she sighed, returning to the present. "So long ago." She opened the wind-eye. The air lay so heavy and still that she could hardly draw in a breath. The outlines of the cottages which lined the lane into the center of Boxton were barely visible in the light of early dawn.

As Rose walked through the awakening village she was amazed at her calmness. *Have I already buried him in my mind?* she wondered. She had never felt so empty of feeling. Her legs seemed wooded, and as she neared the White Horse she had to force them to move. *The part must be played,* she thought. *No escape.* The sky was overcast, but there was enough sun filtering through the clouds to make the cobblestones of High Street glisten. When she turned the corner and approached the entrance to the inn, she saw the sheriff's officers just leaving. She slipped behind a building until they were out of sight.

Cecily peeked out and beckoned to her. Once inside the inn, she was overcome with the desire to see Derick, to touch him.

"Where—?" She looked around frantically.

"Upstairs in a bedchamber," Cecily said softly, "but stay"—she laid her hand on Rose's arm—"Chris is upstairs bribing the guard. Wait here until he signals to you."

There was a roaring fire with bundles of faggots heaped near it. Cecily gestured toward them.

"Chris has been tending the fire all night to dry out the wood so it will catch fire quickly—oh, God's mercy, Rose!" She turned away.

Rose watched the leaping flames. *Bright, cheery fire,* she mused. *We warm ourselves by it on a cold winter night. We use its heat to cook our food, and dance in its light on Midsummer's Eve. Kindly flames. They can lick the flesh off a man and blacken his bones—*

"Did you not hear me?" Cecily was trying to thrust something into her hands. "You are to conceal this and take it up to Derick," she whispered. She gave her a little cloth bag tied up with a long leather thong. "Tell him to wear it inside his shirt so the sheriff won't see."

Rose turned it over in her hand and then asked flatly, "Gunpowder?" Cecily bit her lip and nodded. Rose hid the bag in the folds of Derick's shirt. Chris came downstairs and motioned for her to go up.

As she passed him on the first step he whispered, "We'll keep a watch down here, and when the officers return, the guard will rap on the door to the bedchamber. Go out quickly and hide in one of the other rooms until they have taken Derick out. If they catch you with him, we shall all be in trouble."

Friend, she thought scornfully, *for all your blustering loyalty, your own neck is very dear to you.*

Upstairs the guard stood aside and let her into the room where Derick was held. Derick was stripped to the waist, bending over the washbasin and did not hear her enter. *Oh, God, he's so thin! And those terrible scars!* She flinched at the sight of the bright pink slashes across his back.

"Derick."

He turned around, and she was stunned by the look of anguish in his red-rimmed eyes. She hesitated, then ran and threw her arms around his neck and placed her cheek against his chest. He kept his hands at his sides.

"Oh, your poor back. Did I hurt you?" She clasped his hands and looked up into his face. He looked away as he spoke.

"Nay, you could never hurt me. I —you should not have come," he blurted out. He wrenched his hands from her grasp.

To fill the awkward moment, she stooped and picked up the shirt and bag of gunpowder which had fallen to the ground when she embraced him.

"See, your shirt's all nicely mended," she chattered nervously. "They're drying the wood downstairs. They've dried it all night, and Chris made this bag of gunpowder. Here, here let me tie it on and —" She hugged him fiercely. "Don't die, don't die. Tell them you recant. Tell them whatever they want to hear, only live—live! Please, please, I beg you!" she fell down at his feet.

Derick knelt down beside her and cupped her face in his hands. "Rose, my dearly loved, try to understand—" he began.

"Understand? I cannot understand. You say the mass is idolatrous. Why can you not bow to a thousand idols if it will save your life? What is so evil in the Romish church that you would rather die than praise it?"

"Oh, for the time to tell," he said in exasperation. "They've built a wall of ritual between God and simple folk. The Church denies us the right to study God's Word for ourselves. The mass is but one of their false teachings. The Romish church teaches the cup and bread become Christ's very blood and body sacrificed anew each time they are partaken of. 'Tis not so. He died once for all, and He arose, and"—he grasped her shoulders—"He dwells within my heart. Oh, trust Him, Rose. He'll take care of you."

"Will He?" she asked harshly, "and will He take care of the child I now bear?" She repented of the words as soon as she spoke them, for she saw the anguish the news of her pregnancy caused him.

Derick covered his face with his hands and moaned. Then he looked at her with tears in his eyes as he said, "The Scriptures speak of another cup, the cup of Christ's suffering. Before His death the Lord prayed that that cup would pass from Him, I'm told. Well, I've prayed too that I would be released. I want to live. I want to hold you, to see our child—I love you so much"—the tears rolled down his cheeks—"but I love God even more. I cannot," he sobbed, "I cannot deny the truth."

Rose realized her defeat. He was willingly on the path to his death, and all she could do was stand by. With a shuddering sigh, she began to stroke his hair. "Good-bye, my sweet husband, good-bye, my very dear." He held her so tightly to him that she felt as if they had but one heartbeat, but she knew it was not so. His heart had been pledged to another.

The guard threw open the door and brusquely ordered her out. Derick helped her up and then quickly put on the wedding shirt. She tried to give him one more kiss but the guard shoved her out and into the next room. As she left she could hear Derick pray, "Father in heaven, take care of them, Rose and the babe. Be my strength this day. Let me die praising your name."

The guard shut the door on her, and she pressed up against it. In a moment she heard footsteps and scuffling and then silence. She went down. Cecily was waiting for her at the foot of the stairs.

"I'll take you home," she said.

"Nay, I must be near to him," Rose said as she brushed passed her friend and hurried outside. She joined a small cluster of villagers following Derick and his guards to the Green. The crowd began to grow, and Rose felt herself being swept along. No one spoke to her, but hands supported her, half carrying her as they neared the Green. She realized that in the safety of numbers they were trying to show her sympathy. The people and the landscape along the way were all a blur to her. The only one she saw clearly was Derick. He wore just his long white shirt and his hose, yet there was such nobility in his bearing. At the edge of the Green she suddenly beheld every detail of the dreaded place with an awful clarity. It was a scene identical to the one in Saffron Walden, except that there was no market. A stake had been set in freshly dug earth in the middle of the Green. The priest was talking to Sheriff Pike near the pulpit. A red-haired little boy who was still in skirts kept running to the stake and kicking it. His mother scooped him up in her arms, and as she carried him past Rose she paused, started to say something, then looked away and hurried by her.

The villagers began to encircle the execution site. There were angry murmurs as Derick was tied to the stake. Chris must have carted the bundles of faggots to the Green while Rose was with Derick, for he shoved aside the officer who was laying wood and began carefully laying around Derick the wood he had brought as if he were laying it on his own hearth. After he placed the last of it about him, he placed reeds and straw among the cords that bound Derick. Then he embraced him, his huge arms encircling both Derick and the stake.

Rose tried to run to him, but someone held her back. The priest began his mandatory sermon. She heard none of it. All her being strained to drink in this last glimpse of her husband. He paid no heed to the preaching but had his face turned toward the clouding sky. "He does it all for you," she angrily prayed. "If you cared at all you would cause a mighty deluge and keep the fire from being lit. You would spirit him away—" Just then the torch was lit, and the officer went toward the stake with it. Derick strained forward against his bonds and looked at Rose. Curious faces turned to watch her. She was screaming and knew it not.

Chapter Nine

A STREAM OF ALE from an overturned mug ran along Rose's arm to the edge of the table and dripped onto her skirt, forming a puddle in her lap before spilling onto the rushes of the floor of the cottage. Rose didn't bother to move her arm or dam the stream of ale. She knew that if she moved her arm she would have to stand up; if she stood up she would have to open the shutters; if she opened the shutters she would have to acknowledge that another day had begun, another day without Derick.

She glanced through the doorway into the bedchamber. The coverlet lay twisted over the side of the bed. *Mayhap I could sleep now. There's noise enough outside with the cart wheels and oxen's hooves upon the cobblestones. I might not hear the crackling of the flames that roars in my head each time I close my eyes. Oh, if I could but sleep and never wake. Why did they not just let me die?*

She could neither remember being carried home screaming and raving as the torch lit Derick's pyre, nor being held down by Alice and Cecily as she tried to run back to the Green. But when Chris had come to tell the women it was finished, that Derick was dead, she recalled covering her ears with her hands and running past them out of the cottage, down the path to the fields, just as lightning cracked the sky and a heavy downpour began. On and on she had run in the blinding rain, heedless of the stones and thorns that gashed the soles of her feet. The last thing she remembered was tripping over a log and falling into a muddy ditch by a barley field.

Chris and Barnabe had searched for her until nightfall. When she had come to, the morning sun on her face, Chris was wiping the mud from her eyelids with his kerchief. Everything went black, and then the fever had come. Her bones felt on fire, and she thought her eyes would melt in their sockets. The pain—the hot, red agony—swirled behind her eyes.

"Eat, you must eat for the sake of the child." Voices ordering her, fingers forcing her lips apart, pouring liquid down her throat. Days passed and gradually, her mind cleared, but she would not speak. The pity and love in her friends' eyes would almost compel her to weep, to reach out for their sympathy, but she dared not respond to their kindness. She must keep a wall between herself and the world. To get on with living seemed a sacrilege.

I am a rock, a dead, empty thing. The child within me surely must be dead also. She looked at the sharp bread knife lying on the table beside a moldy loaf. Alice had forgotten to take it with her on her last visit. *I could slash my wrists and watch the blood spill onto my skirt just as I am watching the ale. An easy death.* A fly buzzed around her face. It landed on her arm, and in spite of herself she whisked it away. She sighed and stood up, leaning on the table to steady herself.

"Open to me, Rose," Alice bellowed as she banged on the door.

Rose did not move.

"Mark you, if you do not open this door, I am going to break the shutters and climb through the wind-eye."

Rose visualized Alice stuck halfway through the wind-eye with her arms flailing wildly on the inside of the cottage and her fat legs kicking in the air on the outside, but she did not allow herself to smile. Instead, she walked slowly to the door, opened it and blinked in the glare of the midmorning sun.

"Poor dove," cooed Alice. "Look at those swollen eyes begging to release their tears. When will you give way to the sorrow within you, child? Your heart can never mend 'til then." She took Rose by the arm and steered her to the bench. "Let me comb your hair for you. Tut, I see you haven't touched that nice loaf I brought over. Did you eat the chicken?" She sniffed and made a face. "Never mind, I can smell it." She opened the ambry and, using the end of a broom, shoved the rotten chicken, crawling with maggots, into a bucket.

"I'll cast this out while you put on your other gown." When Alice returned Rose was still sitting on the bench, staring at the cold hearth. "Come, child," Alice said gently, "I'll dress you."

Rose allowed Alice to lead her into the bedchamber and tidy her up as a mother would tend a child. All the while Rose kept her mind floating somewhere above her head.

"I am a rock," she repeated to herself, "a thing that cannot be hurt."

"Now, 'tis market day," said Alice, "and we are going out. It will be well to let the village see that you are feeling better. Cruel are the tongues that wag," she muttered under her breath. When she had tied a cap over Rose's hair she said, "Cecily will meet us in the market square. We shall have a nice time together, and then the two of us will help you put the cottage to right."

Alice kept up a nervous chatter as she led Rose down High Street. Many villagers avoided them, but when confronted face to face, the miller touched his cap and mumbled, "Good to see you about, Mistress—er, Widow Haler."

When they entered the crowded market square, Rose let the stares of the villagers pass through her. Glaring at the curious onlookers, Alice led her to a quiet corner at the end of a row of stalls. Barnabe Coates was waiting there.

"Barnabe, dearest, you look pale," said Alice, her brow wrinkled with concern. "If I could but cook for you again, I'd fatten you up in no time."

"I'm well enough, wife," he whispered the word. "My eyes have been bothering me, though. I can't seem to do any work except in the bright sunlight." He turned to Rose. "My, but you look comely this day," he told her. When she failed to respond he raised his eyebrows at Alice.

"Oh, Rose is doing well, very well," said Alice with contrived cheerfulness. "A few more days, and I'm certain she'll be her old self."

*"Old self!" What was my "old self" except a part of Derick and he a part of me? Alas, my only love is gone and there's no grave to mourn at—no earthy bed to deck with summer flowers and rings of winter holly. That place—that awful place—*She looked toward the village Green—*Has grass grown o'er the spot? Do children play at ball upon his ashes? I cannot go—I must—*

"Ah ha, sister, and where are your three witnesses?" Widow Terrel said as she joined the group. "You know you are not allowed to speak to your former husband without three witnesses at market."

"Look around at the witnesses, sister," retorted Alice. "We are in a public place."

"A cozy, quiet corner, you mean," said the Widow.

Barnabe opened his mouth but Alice gave him a look, and he gritted his teeth and contented himself with a growl.

"Besides," continued Alice, "Rose is here with us."

"Ah, yes, Rose." The widow set down a little pail which she had been carrying. "If you hadn't been so busy helping the poor wretch, I wouldn't have had to come to market myself to buy cream. How can you, a nun, befriend a heretic's wife?"

Alice ignored her and beckened to Cecily who was peering in their general direction. "Ho, Cecily, 'tis us."

Cecily scurried over. "Sorry to be late, but I couldn't see—oh, pardon!"

"You blind oaf!" cried the Widow. "You've knocked over the cream pail—and just look at my shoes!"

"How clumsy of me," said Cecily. "Here, let me help you." She wiped off the Widow's shoes with the hem of her own skirt. When she stood up she looked vacantly around. "But where is Rose?"

"Look, she's going toward the Green," said Barnabe. "I'll stop her."

Alice took his arm. "Nay, love, let her be. This may be what she's needing. Come, we'll follow slowly."

Rose ran up the path. She had dreaded this moment, but something urged her on. The spring rains had brought up a lush new growth of grass over all the open area except for a small bare circle—the place where Derick died. Rose knelt down in the circle and began clawing the hard, soot-blackened crust of earth. By the time her friends reached her she had plowed up the top layer of dirt with her hands and was on her knees, sifting it through her fingers.

"Look at her," whispered Alice to Barnabe and Cecily. "Dear Mother of Heaven, why is she doing that?"

Cecily knelt down beside Rose and grabbed her hands. "Stop, Rose. Stop! What are you looking for?"

"His bones. I must find his bones. They don't all burn, you know." Rose pulled her hands away and began clawing the dirt again. "Help me, Cecily. You too, Alice. I have nothing left of him. I have to find his bones." She lay down in the blackened earth. "Oh, Derick," she sobbed, "I couldn't even bury you."

Alice motioned for Barnabe to leave, and she and Cecily sat by Rose as she wept, pouring out all her pent-up grief. At last she sat up and wiped her face with her sleeve.

"How long ago—" she asked haltingly, "how long ago did he die?"

"Four weeks ago come Saturday," said Alice.

Rose stood up, shook the dirt from her gown and tucked a strand of hair back under her cap. "Now, my dear, kind friends—I want to go home."

Chapter Ten

FROM THAT DAY, just as Alice had predicted, Rose began to recover—if not in her heart, at least in her mind and body. She still could not face the long nights with the empty space beside her where Derick used to lie. She spent most of her daylight hours toiling in her garden and would fall asleep at night wrapped in the coverlet on the houseroom floor.

One brilliant June morning as she was on her knees in the garden, Rose was conscious of the slight swelling in her abdomen. "So you are growing in spite of everything," she told her unborn child. "Well, I am growing good herbs to nourish you, and there'll be cucumbers and gourds, and pompione. 'Ere you're born in November's cold, I'll have laid by plenty to give you wholesome milk. And I've sown some basil in that earthen pot. 'Tis good for sorrowful hearts, they say, it—oh, why must he hammer so loudly?"

She had rented the smithy to the son of a blacksmith from a nearby village who did not want to work with his father. He had agreed to hire Ned to help him, and of that she was glad, but now she repented of her action, for the noise from the smithy only reminded her of Derick. Not that there were no other reminders, she admitted. "Someday a village gossip will take you on the Green and tell you how your father perished," she told the unborn child. "His death may even be acted out before your very eyes," she grimly added.

Even as she spoke, a shadow fell in front of her. As she raised her head she saw first a pair of spindly legs in hose of Lincoln green, and then she found herself staring into the glassy eyes of two dead chickens.

"Good-day to you, Widow Haler." Seward Posthumous Potter stood before her dressed in his Sabbath clothes. He was holding the chickens by their feet, and he thrust them in her face. "I've come to pay my condolences and to bring you these."

"Mmmm," she muttered and continued weeding, hoping he would go away.

Potter cleared his throat. "Can we not go inside? The s-sun is quite warm this morning," he stuttered. The smell of manure from the fields radiated from him. *He's old enough to be my father, nay, my grandfather,* she thought, *but I know well enough why he's come.* Potter owned the land which had adjoined her aunt's farm. Years ago, on his visits to her aunt, he had always fussed over Rose, bringing her sweets and attempting to obtain a kiss in payment. She had thought him repulsive and would hide in the fields when she saw him coming.

"Please, may we go in?" he persisted.

She sighed and brushed the dirt from her hands. *I must be civil to him,* she grudgingly admitted. It was the only way to get rid of him—and besides, she could use the chickens. "Very well," she replied, "we shall go in, but just for a moment."

Inside, he plopped the chickens down upon her clean table and settled himself on the bench.

"My heartfelt s-sympathy," he began. "It must be very difficult for you."

"I manage."

"I passed by your fields on my way into the village. They are in s-sad shape, I'm afraid." He leered at her. "They want a man to oversee them." He surveyed the houseroom. "This little cottage is s-sound. Has the s-smith who rents the sm-smithy money to purchase it and the cottage?"

Land-hungry lecher, she thought, and started for the door. "I must get back to my gardening, Master Potter," she said aloud. He came up behind her, his foul breath warm on the back of her neck.

"S-so young a widow and s-so comely," he stammered. "S-sit with me and let me ease your s-sorrow." He grabbed her clumsily around the waist and sat down on the bench, pulling her onto his lap. She wrestled herself from his grasp, and Potter lost his balance, falling sideways onto the floor. She laughed heartily and was still laughing as he limped away.

But after a moment she wiped her eyes with her apron and cried out angrily, "Oh, Derick, how could you leave me to endure this?"

A week later, she asked Cecily in disgust, "Is that all I am to be now, just so much meat on the market?" She was working in her garden again. "Seven weeks a widow, and I've received three proposals of marriage."

"Two others beside old, amorous Potter?" asked Cecily.

"Aye," said Rose, jabbing the earth with her trowel. "The miller came by and without preface asked me to be his helpmeet and a mother for his six children. And Master Brian—"

"Him?" Cecily was incredulous. "That ancient, palsied bag of bones asked you to wed?"

"Hmph. He fixed his rheumy eye on me and said, 'I need you for my wife, you lusty girl.' 'You need a nurse, not a wife,' I answered, and closed the door on him."

Cecily held her sides, and roared with laughter.

" 'Tis not laughable," muttered Rose as she stood up.

"Forgive me, friend." Cecily tried to look serious. "There are suitors more worthy to be considered. I've heard of a goodly yeoman near Saffron Walden who is looking for a wife."

"But I'm not looking to wed," said Rose.

"A woman shouldn't be alone, especially one who carries a child," Cecily said firmly. "You need a man who'll take care of you."

"I had the only man I ever wanted. Oh, Cecily, how could he do this to me? How could he die and leave me to the mercy of slobbering suitors?" She choked back tears and continued, "I have made a decision. I am going to leave Boxton. No—" she said over her friend's protests, "my mind is set. As long as I stay here I will smell the smoke from that day. Besides, I cannot abide seeing her—" She gestured toward the Widow Terrel's cottage.

"Most of the village is shunning her," said Cecily. "Chris said there's talk of making rough music at her door some night."

"Bah! 'Tis empty talk," Rose replied. "No one really cares. They but play at retribution."

"But where will you go? Who will take care of you?"

"I will take care of myself," Rose answered, as she pulled herself up to her full height. "At least until I find my brother, Robin. I'll sell everything and go up to London. My brother is still there, somewhere. It should not be too hard to find him, and when I do, we can live together."

"But London, Rose—" Cecily protested. " 'Tis a wondrous wicked place. The streets are full of beggars and cutpurses, and there are harmful vapors in the air. 'Twould be a terrible town to birth a child in."

Rose smiled. "You forget that I was born there. Nay, 'twill be a good place to start a new life. And there, no one has heard of—the tragedy. My child will learn to be a printer."

"If it be a male child."

" 'Tis a son, I know it. And he will not spend his life in a backward village full of hard hearts."

"I am not hard of heart, friend," said Cecily gently.

"Truly you are not," Rose warmly answered, "Nor Chris nor Alice nor Barnabe. As for the rest"—she looked toward the Green—"well, the sooner I leave them behind, the better."

Rose sold the cottage, smithy, and land to Seward Posthumous Potter the very next day. He signed the papers reluctantly, sighing with regret that she was not thrown into the bargain. At her urging, Chris found a yeoman traveling to London with his family to visit relatives and they welcomed Rose to journey with them.

On the evening before she was to leave, Rose lingered in the doorway of the cottage. It was dusk, the homing time, when families gathered and fires were lit and the cares of the day eased away. She was overcome with loneliness as she stared at the path which led to the smithy and remembered how Derick looked as he hastened in to supper after a long hard day at the anvil. *'Twas a goodly choice I made. How could I stay with these remembered moments tugging at my heart?* She glanced at the herb garden she had tended so carefully. Few of the plants were thriving, for this promised to be as dry a summer as the last was wet. *That must be an omen dark. My child would never thrive in this place.*

She tried to fight off depression by listing the chores for her departure. The furniture was sold with the cottage to Master Potter. The household things she left to Cecily, and what she did not need would be dispersed to the poor. "I'll scour the last cooking pot tonight," she decided.

"The Bible!" she exclaimed. "What's to be done? I'll bury it, as I should have done long ago. To think that the Scriptures read by my own lips helped Derick make his deadly stand." She waited until it was completely dark, and then began digging in her garden.

"Whatever are you doing?" a voice whispered behind her.

"Oh, Alice, you frighted me!" She pointed to the Bible which lay on the ground, "I'm putting this where it will do no more harm."

Alice stooped and picked the Book up. "The Holy Scriptures, in our native tongue. I've never read them," she said wistfully. She began to leaf through the pages, and then she quickly closed the cover. " 'Tis forbidden—still—. Rose—" her voice pitched with excitement—"give this Bible to me."

"But the danger—your sister—"

"Fie upon her. She may be cunning, but I'm her mother's daughter, also. I shall closet the Scriptures where she will never find them. God's very words—I've longed to read them for myself."

Finally Rose gave in, and after Alice had hidden the volume in the folds of her habit, she bade her a tearful farewell.

The next morning, Rose dressed quickly at dawn. She gathered the few things she would take with her: her Sabbath gown, her mother's silver thimble, and the little wrought-iron bird Derick had fashioned for her. All these she placed in the linen bag she would carry. Money from the sale of her property was in a little purse she tied to her waist.

After a last look around, she went out, closing the cottage door softly. Smoke was already rising from the smithy—the young smith was industrious. Rose's new shoes, a parting gift from Barnabe, clapped against the cobblestones as she walked down High Street toward the crossroads where she would join the yeoman and his family. A few of the village dogs rushed out barking when they heard footsteps, but they wagged their tails when they recognized her.

She would be known to neither man nor beast in London, she realized, save for her brother. And what if he had died? What if he could not afford to take her in? "You're beginning to sound like Cecily," she told herself, "always worrying. Well, 'tis done, the house is swept clean, and there's no turning back."

She hesitated as she neared the church. "Nay, I'll not go near the babies' beds," she decided. Cecily had promised to tend the graves and set flowers out on special days.

She walked on rapidly past the White Horse. She had made her farewell to Chris and Cecily the day before. Averting her eyes, she took the long way around the Green. She wished to see it no more.

Her fellow travelers were waiting for her at the crossroads. Besides the yeoman, his wife and children, five servants accompanied the group to protect them from highwaymen. Rose stopped just once to look back as they made their way down the road toward London. Above the hedgerow she could just see the spire of the village church. But it was not Boxton she regretted leaving.

"Good-bye, my love, my only love," she whispered. Then she turned her back and hurried down the road toward London. Had she known the danger that awaited her in that new life, she might not have hastened so quickly toward it.

Chapter Eleven

AT THE END of the first day, the travelers made camp in a field near the side of the road. Rose bedded down with the yeoman's wife and daughter. The young girl had been watching her furtively all day, and after her mother had fallen asleep she whispered, "Madam, are you not terrified to be leaving your village?"

Rose merely smiled and shook her head, but as she gazed up at the stars, she began to sort out her feelings. She *was* a little afraid, she admitted to herself, but compared to the terrible dread she had endured during Derick's imprisonment, this fear of the unknown was light indeed. As for sorrow, she would always bear it, wear it as a heavy mantle. But she felt something else—a vague, unsettling emotion. When the realization suddenly came to her, she was almost overwhelmed with guilt. For the first time in many months, she was facing the future with glad anticipation—and part of the pleasure, the part that shamed her, was that she was on her own, independent for the first time in her life. "Oh, Derick, forgive me!" she cried inwardly, and willed his face to appear in her mind until she slept.

By noon the next day Rose could see London in the distance. In her memory, Rose had always envisioned the city as standing apart in the midst of a green countryside, its walls and spires gleaming in the sun. Instead, she saw a sprawling suburb with ramshackle cottages and boggy fields that draped around the city like a filthy skirt. A smoky haze hung over the city's rooftops. Since they were approaching from the north and east of the walled city, there was no view of the Thames River or the magnificent bridge which spanned it, nor of the moated Tower of London where the Princess Elizabeth had been imprisoned by her sister, Mary.

Rose was even more dismayed when they entered through

Bishopsgate. Rows of dingy houses lined the narrow lanes. An overwhelming stench rose from the gutter.

"Heads up!" a woman shouted from the jettied floor above a shop they were passing. The contents of a chamber pot splashed on Rose's shoes as the woman dumped it from the second story windeye. By the time the party reached their destination, a house on Threadneedle Street, Rose's anticipation of independence had dulled. She now felt faint and full of doubts. There were so many streets, so many people! How could she hope to find her brother? Somewhere in view of the huge spire of St. Paul's Cathedral she had lived with her parents and Robin in the rooms above her father's shop. That memory and the fact that Robin was a printer were all she had to go on. "Have I played the fool?" she asked herself as she rested in the parlor.

"You are quite welcome to spend the night with us," the yeoman's sister offered. "I'm certain my brother would escort you through the city on the morrow."

Rose refused her kind offer. The small house would be overcrowded as it was, and she knew the yeoman would not wish to spend his holiday acting as her guide. After she had been given directions to St. Paul's, she began walking, carrying the bag which contained all her possessions. She slipped the purse which was tied to her waist inside her skirt. As she walked along Cheapside Street, she took care not to step in the refuse piled in front of every dwelling. Some of the London women, she noticed, had found a solution to the perilous travel: they walked about on tall wooden platforms which were tied to their shoes.

The city was hot, much hotter than the village. Here there was no space between the houses, no flowered gardens to scent the air. She walked past food stalls. "Pies, hot pies!" one vendor called. The smell of food combined with the stench of the drainage ditch was overpowering. She felt dizzy. "Perhaps I should stop and fill my stomach," she considered. She pulled out her purse and, counting out twopence, purchased a meat pie and stood in the shade of an awning to eat it.

Suddenly, a man passing by tripped and fell against her, almost causing her to fall. "My pardon, lady," he said as he doffed his dirty cap and bowed. "Did I harm you?"

"Nay, sir, you did not," she replied, thinking that at least these city dwellers were courteous, if clumsy.

"Good-day to you, then," he answered and jauntily swept his short cape about him as he hurried off.

The pie vendor leaned on his counter and asked her contemptuously, "Country bumpkin, ain't you?"

She looked at him blankly. He spat on the ground and said, "Your purse, fool."

She felt for her purse and touched the cut cord dangling from her waist.

"He stole it," the victualler nodded in the direction of the fleeing man, "Cut it clean off when he stumbled into you."

"Stop, thief!" Rose called out frantically, but the man had already disappeared into the crowd on the busy street.

"He'll go off in some alley and count your pennies."

"But what will I do? 'Tis all the money I had—" Rose began, but the victualler had already turned his back on her. Several people had stopped to watch her predicament, but when she looked into their faces, no one met her glance. *Mother of Mercy,* she thought, *will no one aid me?* She looked beseechingly around at the bystanders again, and this time one returned her gaze. She could tell by his velvet plumed hat and the gold chain that clasped his russet cloak that he must be a gentleman. He eyed Rose, picking his teeth with an ivory pick. As she was about to turn from him, he stepped forward and bowed low.

"Giles Winthrop at your service, madam. May I be of assistance?"

Rose sighed with relief. "Oh, sir, I wist not what to do. I have come to the city to find my long-lost brother and now all my money has been stolen." She choked back tears, and he gallantly offered her an embroidered handkerchief which had been tucked in his sleeve. He continued looking her over as she told him about Robin. She knew she was talking too fast and telling a stranger too much, but in her state of panic she could not stop. The other bystanders had lost interest in her plight and had gone on their way.

When Rose finally finished her story, Winthrop took her arm and said, "Allow me to escort you to Stationers' Hall. No doubt they must have the address of every printer in London. If we cannot find your brother by nightfall, I will then conduct you to the Sisters of Charity. They will give you lodging for the night. Come along, then." He widened his solicitous smile and tightened his grip on her arm.

She hesitated and thought, *I shouldn't trust him.* She looked around and considered—it was still quite light and there were so many people on the streets—very well, she would go with him but keep on her guard. "Thank you, sir," she said. "I will accept your kind offer."

Master Winthrop led her away from broad Cheapside and down a narrow lane. His talk was so entertaining that she did not realize he was leading her away from the center of London and toward the river until they were almost at the water's edge. She could see London Bridge a few hundred yards up river. The huge bridge with its twenty arches spanning the Thames looked to her like more of a market than a bridge. There were few spaces across its expanse that were not filled by buildings.

"Stationers' Hall, 'tis across the river?" she asked Winthrop.

"Aye," he said shortly and jerked her arm, propelling her down river.

"But the bridge is in the other direction—" Rose began to feel afraid.

"The bridge is too crowded with shops and houses," he answered and smiled coldly down at her. "I'll hire a wherry to take us across."

She could see several of the small skiffs carrying passengers across the river to the Southwark side and so she relaxed again as he led her toward an enclosed wherry which was bobbing by the bank.

The wherryman was asleep on the stair-foot, and Winthrop gave him a sound kick. "Awake, you wastrel!" he ordered, "and carry us to Southwark."

The wherryman jumped up and squinted at Rose as he said, "Ah, Master Giles, you've made a fair catch today."

"Catch? What means he?" she asked Winthrop as her heart began pounding.

"Stay, stay, Mistress," Winthrop said soothingly as he gave the wherryman a threatening look. "The scoundrel but implied I had found a comely companion.—Here, you insolent wretch! No more of your talk in the presence of a gentlewoman." At that, the wherryman bowed and helped them aboard.

As the little skiff was rowed across the river, Rose felt a growing uneasiness. *I've been a fool,* she told herself, *allowing a perfect stranger to lead me about. Once we're ashore, I'll take my leave and find a refuge. Surely there are kind townspeople who will take pity on a poor sojourner.* But when they disembarked in Southwark, her heart sank. Instead of kindly townsmen, she saw two men brawling in the street and a sailor staggering down to retch into the river. Wild laughter came from a bawdy house a short distance away.

"Of a truth, good sir, I can make my own way now," she began, her voice rising with fear.

Winthrop grabbed Rose around the waist and turned her so that his body would shield her from the view of anyone in the buildings which lined the riverbank. To a passerby it would appear that he was embracing her. "Harken to me, wench," he said roughly under his breath. "I am going to do you a service. You have neither money nor home, and I can provide you with both." His eyes narrowed and he smiled coldly down at her. "But instead of a brother, I shall give you a mother." He laughed at his own cleverness. "Yes, Mother Gaines will welcome you with loving arms." Rose flinched as he caressed her cheek. "Mother pays me well to find her fair wenches for her stewhouse."

"A brothel!" Rose gasped and tried to wrench herself from his grasp. Her heart was pounding furiously as she struggled to get free. "Fool, fool, fool," she told herself as she looked wildly about for aid, but the only one who noticed her plight was the wherryman who was leaning on his oar and smiling broadly.

She felt something sharp prick her throat. "Behold," he said as he held a stiletto up to her face. It was partially concealed in the end of his cloak but she could see its long sharp point. "This is my little carver. One false move and it will slice open your gullet. Now come." He hid his knife and held her tightly by the arm as they walked along Bankside.

Rose fought down panic. She saw nothing but stewhouses. Women were lounging in doorways calling out to the few sailors on the path. If she cried out, she doubted anyone would come to her aid. *If I could just take him off guard*—Rose staggered and fell against him, pretending to faint. He pulled her up sharply.

"None of your tricks," he snarled. "I'll not have my day's work gone for naught." He dug his fingers into the flesh of her arm.

"You're hurting me."

"Be glad I've done no more, madam. A few more yards and I'll be rid of you." He dragged her forward, and she could see a building ahead emblazoned with "Mother Gaines and Her Cherries Ripe" in red paint across the doorway.

Rose steeled herself for one more attempt at escaping. "Forgive me, my baby, my dearling," she told her unborn child, "but I would rather die than see you born to a dishonored mother in a bawdy house."

Just as Rose readied herself for flight an off-key trumpet sounded, and a man stepped out of an alleyway into their path. He carried a placard announcing a bearbaiting, and behind him followed the drunken trumpeter and five sailors walking arm in arm. Winthrop was forced to pull Rose back into a doorway to let them pass. There was a low growl, and Rose shrieked inadvertently as she saw the huge brown bear being led behind. The bear was walking on its hind feet, and although it was muzzled, its massive claws looked capable of inflicting deadly injury.

As the bear passed in front of them, a black and white terrier rushed from the doorway in which they were standing and stood between Winthrop's legs, barking at the bear. Winthrop started to kick the dog out of his way, but the bear lunged toward him, trying to attack the dog. As Winthrop released Rose to ward off the bear's menacing paws, she shoved past the bearkeeper and ran toward the bridge.

"Help me! God, help me!" she pleaded as she dashed toward the bridge. Her left side ached, and her lungs felt as if they would burst, but she plunged on. The street became more crowded as she neared the bridge, and people watched her curiously or cursed her as she lunged past them. Just as she reached the bridge, she slipped on a melon rind in the littered street and went sprawling on her face in the dirt. Hands grabbed her by the shoulders and helped her to her feet. She turned around slowly expecting to find Winthrop, but gazed instead into the wizened face of an old friar. He had pulled out a cloth from his robes and offered it to her to wipe her face, but she turned, and calling a swift "thank you," over her shoulder, hurried onto the bridge and was swallowed up in the throng.

The narrow path between the houses and shops which lined the bridge throbbed with pedestrians, but Rose pushed her way through as fast as she could. She expected any moment to feel Winthrop's breath on her neck or his sharp knife in her back. About halfway across, she was shoved by the mass of travelers toward the open door of a shop. Above the entrance was a sign which read "A. Denley, Mercer." On impulse she rushed inside. She stood for a moment inside the doorway to get her breath. She saw bolts of fabric of every color on shelves against the wall, and at the counter, waiting on a customer, stood the tallest woman Rose had ever seen. She was quite comely, Rose thought, despite her height, and she looked at Rose with piercing pale blue eyes.

What must she think of me? Rose wondered, blushing. Bedraggled, cap askew, muck from the street on her face—she half expected the shopkeeper to chase her out. Instead, the woman excused herself from her customer and beckoned Rose to follow her into a back room.

"What misfortune has befallen you, poor girl?" she asked Rose.

"Oh, madam, can you help me? Someone stole my purse and

then this horrible man—" Forgetting her first mistake in confiding in a stranger, Rose blurted out the whole adventure to the woman.

When she finished her tale she began to shiver, and the woman patted her shoulder. "There, now, you're safe here.—Hugh! Hugh!" she called. A burly man came in. He was not as tall as his mistress, but he made up for it in width. "I am Joan Denley and I own this shop. This is Hugh, my steward," she told Rose. "Now, you describe the varlet to Hugh, and he'll stand watch outside and handle him if he comes near. My guess, though, is that you will never see the vermin again. His like are brave enough when they are frightening a helpless woman, but they disappear into the gutter if there's a chance they themselves might come to harm." She turned to the steward. "Hugh, after—what are you called, dear?"

"Rose, Rose Haler." She began to relax in the calm strength that seemed to flow from Joan.

"After Rose gives you the knave's description," Joan continued, "get one of the maids to escort her to the topmost bedchamber. I must get back to my customers." She gripped Rose's hand. "Rest for a while. We can talk later."

Rose tried to thank her, but she waved her hand. " 'Tis nothing. We women must stick together against this wicked world."

A maid showed Rose up to a neat little bedchamber. A few moments later she stretched out on the down mattress and promptly fell asleep.

Chapter Twelve

WHEN ROSE AWOKE, morning sunlight was streaming in the small wind-eye. For a moment she could not remember where she was. As she sat up, rubbing her eyes, she heard not the quiet country sounds of Boxton, but footsteps, peddlers' cries, and an unfamiliar swishing sound, all coming from somewhere below. "London Bridge!" she exclaimed, remembering. She rushed to the wind-eye and stood on tiptoe for a good view of the Thames River. Her bed-chamber must be on the eastern side of the bridge, for she could see not only wherries and barges but also several large sailing ships in the distance as they made their way toward the ocean. There was a tap on the door.

"Come in," she called.

A serving girl entered, carrying a jug of water. "Good morning, madam," she said curtsying. "My mistress begs you join her for breakfast."

As she entered the hall, Rose stared, openmouthed, at the great array of food on the dining table. There were saffron cakes, three kinds of cheese, bacon, smoked herring, light bread, eggs and dried fruits—all handsomely displayed on pewter plates. Joan was sitting at the head of the table, daintily wiping grease from her chin. She belched contentedly. "Sit you down, Rose, and fill your belly." She gestured to the chair on her right. "Have some of this, and this, and this," she said, heaping Rose's plate. Joan watched her intently as she ate, and Rose self-consciously picked at her breakfast. After a few bites, however, she realized how famished she really was and soon cleaned her plate.

"Good—I like to see victuals enjoyed," Joan said approvingly. "Now, you've acquainted me with your frightening experience in

Southwark, but how came you alone to London in the first place?"

Rose told her about Derick's death and of her desire to find her brother. As she spoke, she watched Joan's face for any sign of shock. After all, she thought, Joan was learning that she had offered refuge to a heretic's wife. But Joan showed no emotion except sympathy, and when Rose finished her story she merely murmured, "Ah, 'tis a sorry state of affairs when Englishmen put fire to their own countrymen."

"Are you a widow also?" Rose asked. She had seen no sign of a husband. When Joan nodded, Rose blurted out, "Then your husband—was he burned at the stake, also?" That would account for Joan's sympathy.

"Bless you, no! He was too cautious a man to have opinions about religion, especially dangerous opinions. Nay, he died of natural causes, if you can call being cut on by a harebrained barber a natural cause." She picked up an apple and began to peel it slowly. "He was hauling in a barrel of imported cloth and dropped it on his foot. The foot swelled up something fearful and turned black." She paused for a long drink of ale. "I sent for the barber, and he said the foot must come off. The dolt did the job well enough, but he had drunk more wine than we had pumped into my old man, and he failed to cauterize the wound properly. My old man's lifeblood squirted out all over this room. He thrashed about like a chicken with its head cut off, and by the time we caught him he had lost too much blood." She laughed heartily and then peered at Rose. "What's the matter, dear? You look pale as a ghost."

" 'Tis just—forgive me, but how can you jest about so horrible a dying?"

"Ah, well, my friend, I'd rather laugh than cry." Joan wiped her eyes with her sleeve. "Besides, whichever I do, he is still dead"—she looked into her mug—"as dead as this ale. Tell me now, do you believe as your husband did?" Her pale blue eyes watched Rose closely.

Rose looked down at her hands. "Of a truth, I am mortal tired of all religion. It all had a part in Derick's death. The Catholics lit the fire, but the reformers pushed him to the stake. Yet—yet if I say all religion is vain, that there is no God, or that if He exists He cares not for His own, then I have to admit that Derick died for naught, that his death was as senseless as your husband's—oh, I wist not what I am saying!"

"There, there," Joan said as she patted her hand, "I know your meaning. I'm not a hot gospeller myself. Oh, I attend meetings of the secret coventicle, and I do my bit to help the imprisoned believers, but mainly because I hate the Queen." Her voice hardened. " 'Tis the Lady Elizabeth who should be on the throne and not that woman. Imagine her marrying a *Spaniard*! As for all that popery she has brought back to England, wrap it up and pack it off to Rome, I say. England for the English!" She slammed her fist on the table, rattling the pewter plates.

Hugh the steward came in to tell his mistress he was going to the docks to fetch a shipment of laces from East Friesland. Rose noticed Joan's affectionate glance as he left the room.

"Mayhap, I pry too much," Joan said, "but had you no suitors in your village, as comely a young widow as you are?"

Rose made a face as she recalled Seward Posthumous Potter. "Aye, I had suitors."

"Say no more," Joan said with a smile, "I know too well. As soon as my husband was in the ground, I had my fill of vultures ready to feed upon my wealth." She pushed back her chair and stood up, towering over Rose. "I wasn't eager to divide what my husband and I had worked so hard to earn." She smoothed out her skirts. "I am famous for my imported fabrics. Yea, I've managed quite well. I can trust my servants, especially my steward, and there's no one in London who knows fabrics as well as I." She laughed again. "My pardon—I boast overmuch."

Rose merely smiled. She did not point out the obvious inconsistency with Joan's patriotism. Apparently her love for things English did not extend to cloth made in England when there was money to be earned from foreign goods. Instead she said, "I am truly grateful for your hospitality, but I must not impose on you any longer. Winthrop, that beast, mentioned the Sisters of Charity. Was that another of his lies or will they truly provide lodging for poor travelers?"

"They will, but there's no need. You must stay with me until you find your brother."

"But I cannot pay you. If there's some work I could do—"

"There is. I do need someone to help in the shop," Joan said briskly. "And I'll assist you in finding your brother. 'Tis a pretty puzzle, and I like puzzles. Come along, and I'll set you to work. After the midday meal, I shall have Hugh escort you to your childhood home. You'd best not go out alone again."

Rose shivered as she thought of her harrowing escape from Winthrop.

Joan led her into a storeroom which contained a large sorting table and a row of barrels against the wall. "Unpack the barrels that have been opened," Joan instructed, "and shake out the cloth to make certain no bugs have stowed away on the sea voyage." She shook out a filmy white material to demonstrate, and held it up by the open wind-eye. "Then check it carefully for holes and blemishes. Watch now how I fold it, so."

After Joan left her and went to open the shop, Rose fell to her task with great enthusiasm. She had never seen such beautiful cloth. Each time she pulled out another piece of fabric or lace from a barrel, she was delighted to find a new color or an unusual texture. When she unpacked a fine taffeta, it shimmered in the light. It was the color of a bright summer sky. With a glance toward the doorway to see if anyone was observing, she draped the fabric over her shoulders and looked around for something in which to see her image. On a shelf she found a pewter bowl which held skeins of yarn. She emptied it and held it up before her. *I look beautiful,* she thought, then laughed at her vanity. *Who wouldn't look beautiful wearing such a lovely color?*

Rose heard footsteps and quickly folded the taffeta and placed it on the table. This was the first time she had given so much as a thought to her appearance since Derick's death, and it made her feel as if she were coming alive again. "Tut, vain woman!" she told herself. "You shall be so swollen and misshapen as the babe grows that no one will notice you if you even wear a gown made of butterfly wings."

Hugh came in followed by another male servant. They both carried oaken barrels on their shoulders, and Rose watched as the men set them in the corner. "I wonder what those contain?" she asked herself. "Could the lace from East Friesland be trimmed in gold?" She walked over to the men and said, "If you'll pry the lids off for me, I can unpack the laces before midday."

"Leave them be." Hugh said brusquely over his shoulder. "When Mistress Denley wants them open, she'll tell me."

"But surely she won't mind if I take a peek." He didn't answer her. *Who does he think himself to be?* she fumed. *He isn't master of this house yet.* "I've never seen laces from East Friesland," she said in a reasonable tone. "Are they made in that country or imported from a place even farther away? Are they of gold?"

As she edged nearer, Hugh turned around quickly and blocked her way to the barrels. "Nay," he said, "These be—that is, my mistress—"

"What Hugh means," Joan said from the doorway, "is that these are very special laces, and I prefer to unpack them myself." She paused, and as if realizing how abrupt her words had sounded, smiled sweetly before she asked, "Shall we go to dinner?"

Unpack the whole lot, for all I care, Rose thought, annoyed, as she followed Joan to the table. Even so, curiosity began to rise up within her. What could be so special about those laces that only Joan could handle them?

In the afternoon, as Joan had promised, Hugh escorted Rose in the search for her old home. He walked quickly through the lanes, barely pausing to let her catch up before starting again. From the way he hunched his wide shoulders as he walked and sighed frequently, Rose could tell he begrudged his role. Apparently he felt that his mistress' right-hand man was too important to lead a country girl about.

On her first walk through the city, Rose had been too confused to notice much architecture. Now, however, secure in the company of a guide, she would have enjoyed stopping from time to time to view the fine houses and shops along the way. There was one sight she wished she could not see—the pitiful spectacle of the ragged hollow-eyed beggars who thronged the streets. At some points it was nearly impossible to push through the groups of pleading, whining, cajoling poor. Most heart-rending to Rose was the sight of mothers shuffling along with blank expressions on their faces, trying, it seemed, to block from their minds the hunger of the little children who clung to their skirts. She longed to have bags of money, coins to put into each outstretched hand.

When Hugh led her by St. Paul's, he stopped long enough to allow her to gawk at the huge building with its tall spire.

"Grand, is it not?" These were the first words he had spoken to her directly. "You've nothing like it back in your country village, I ween."

"Nay," she replied, looking up in wonder. " 'Tis strange, but all I recall of St. Paul's from my childhood is its spire. I cannot remember the buildings even though I must have passed by frequently."

"Like as not, your parents didn't allow you to come near the church. A regular den of thieves, it is. Cutpurses and pickpockets do a fat business inside. Farmers coming to town for the first time stand in Paul's Walk and gawk just as you are doing. They leave poorer but wiser for it. If we had time I could show you many fair sights in the churchyard and beyond—the Bishop of London's palace for one. See that tower? 'Tis called Lollard's Tower. No doubt Bishop Bonner even now keeps some imprisoned in it for their faith."

She shivered as she thought of being near the palace of the man who had condemned Derick to death. "Where is Newgate prison?" she asked Hugh.

"Newgate? Oh, in that direction." He waved his arm southward. He had lost interest in his role as guide. "Hasten now. Ave Mary Lane is but a few steps from here."

When they turned down a small lane west of the church, Rose caught her breath. *I remember. This is it, Ave Mary Lane—Home! Down there is the old well with two buckets and there—our house.* It was a timber-and-wattle building with a jettied second floor, similar to others which lined the narrow lane. Before the doorway, where her father had set up his bookstall, a tailor now was seated on a stool, sewing on a green cloak.

"Good-day, sir," she began, "I've come up from Boxton and—"

"What is that to me?" he snapped, pulling the needle through the fabric.

"This used to be my home," she finished in a rush. Her legs were trembling. "Allworth was our family name. By chance did you know my father?"

He sighed and put down his needle. "Nay, I inherited this wretched place from my brother two years past. If it's memories of the past you seek, ask the old apothecary." He pointed to a shop two doors down. "He'll bend the ear of any listener. That's all he's good for these days. His potions will more likely kill than cure." He squinted up at Rose. "Now begone. You're in my light."

Hugh waited impatiently in the shade of an awning while Rose entered the shop. It smelled of strange herbs and decayed flesh. Cobweb-laced shelves were crammed with dusty crocks and jugs. Once inside, Rose faintly remembered the shop. She recalled the fright she once felt when she had waited as her mother purchased a little bag of frankincense to burn to keep away infections. Despite the precaution, her parents had died of fever a short time later.

"Who's there?" A wizened old man in a moth-eaten robe came out from a back room. His face was deeply wrinkled, and sparse tufts of white hair marked his scalp and chin. He shuffled to within a foot of Rose and peered into her face. "Why are you here?" he whined. "No one comes to my shop these days."

"Sir, I am the daughter of John Allworth, the bookseller who lived in this lane years ago." *'Tis hopeless,* she thought. *He'll not remember anything.*

The apothecary faltered to the counter and began grinding a saffron-colored powder. Rose waited for him to speak, but when he said nothing she turned to leave. Suddenly he spoke in a confident voice.

"John Allworth is dead. Died of a fever in King Hal's time."

"'Tis so," she said excitedly. "He was my father."

He looked at her with unbelief. "Nay, his daughter is a tiny lass, no taller than this countertop."

"I am Rose. I've grown up." She spoke slowly as to a young child. "My brother, do you remember him also? His name is Robin."

The apothecary's face lit up. "Fair-haired boy, hair almost as white as snow. A courteous lad. Not like some today who throw stones at me and call me a witch. Why, some of them would never have been born if I hadn't sold their fathers powder from a unicorn's horn—"

"My brother." Rose broke into his reverie.

"Ah, of a truth, an intelligent child. Watched me work and asked all manner of questions. I had intended to ask his father if he would apprentice the boy to me."

"He was apprenticed to a printer after our parents died. Do you remember his name?"

"A printer, eh? After the Allworths died, man and wife, the shop was boarded up, and the lad and little girl were taken away. Stay"—He waved the pestle at her—"I do recall the lad showing up on my doorstep a few months later. Asked if I knew where his sister had been taken. I could tell him nothing of the matter. The boy's master came in and beat him and dragged him away. I never saw the lad again." He went back to his grinding and ignored her completely.

Rose left the shop and beckoned to Hugh to take her back to Joan's. *To think that while I was crying myself to sleep at Auntie's,* she thought, *calling out Robin's name, he was vainly searching this very lane for me.* "Oh, Robin," she whispered, "I'll find you yet. I must."

Chapter Thirteen

THE NEXT DAY was the Sabbath. When Rose went downstairs to breakfast, Joan was about to go out the door, carrying a basket full of bread.

"Oh, good Sabbath," Joan said hurriedly. "Do go in and have your breakfast. I'm taking these loaves to the imprisoned believers in Newgate. When I return, we'll form a plan for finding your brother."

"Let me go with you," Rose said as she reached for her cloak. Although she knew it would be a painful experience, she had a desire to see the place where Derick had been imprisoned.

Joan called to Hugh who had been waiting outside, "I'll just be a moment." Then she closed the door and said softly, "Of a truth, dear, I am going to visit the prison, but there's also a secret meeting of believers today at the house of a Dutch shoemaker. I'd take you along gladly, but there have been informers of late who have given the names of several of the congregation to the authorities. The deacon is very strict about allowing only those on the membership list to worship with us. I shall ask permission to bring you with Hugh and me the next time."

Rose assured her she understood and bade her godspeed. Actually, she had little desire to join heretics in their illegal service. *Joan seemed to enjoy the danger of secret meetings more than the religious experience*, she mused.

By midday Joan had returned to recite her morning's adventures over a joint of mutton. Hugh was seated beside his mistress, much to the consternation of the maid who served them.

" 'Twould fair burst your heart to see the wretches in Newgate Prison thrusting their hands up through the grates, begging for food." This she said between mouthfuls of mutton. "I should have taken more bread.—Hugh, we shall both carry two baskets the next time."

"Does the keeper allow you in?" Rose asked her. "When my husband was imprisoned there, we could not so much as get a message to him."

"Everything has its price—especially at Newgate," Joan said grimly. "What I spend for the privilege of sending Hugh in with the bread, so that we know it does not end up on the keeper's table, would buy ten times as many loaves." She spat out a piece of gristle. "There are nearer prisons, the Clink and the Comptor, for instance, but I've had no luck with bribery at them."

"She makes a sport of it, she does," said Hugh, giving his mistress an admiring glance.

The reminder of Derick's imprisonment cast a pall of gloom around Rose and she pushed her plate aside. "If you'll pardon—" she began, rising.

"Please, stay—" Joan paused to wash down her food with a long drink of cider. "I've saved the best for last. You could have come with us to the meeting today with no trouble at all, for your husband's name is becoming known among believers. Before the sermon was preached—"

"And a long one it was," Hugh interrupted.

"—a young girl sang a newly made ballad of the martyrs. There was a verse I thought would please you.—Hugh?"

Hugh cleared his throat and sang in a surprisingly pleasant voice:

"The blacksmith stood on Boxton's Green
And raised his voice toward heaven.
'I'll take this cup of suffering
That by my Lord is given.' "

Rose bolted from the room. All the sorrow that had been overlaid by the excitement of the past few days had broken through with a torrent of tears. Joan wisely let her alone with her grief; she spent the remainder of that Sabbath in her chamber.

On Monday Joan took Rose to Stationer's Hall in hopes of locating Robin's address. The hall's officers had no record of his indenture, because printers had been a part of the guild only a short time. Neither was there a current listing of Robin as a journeyman printer. " 'Tis hopeless!" Rose exclaimed. "He has moved to another town or changed his trade, or, with a harsh master, he might even have run away to sea. Tomorrow I'll take my leave," she told Joan.

"I cannot live off your kindness any longer."

"Silence, girl," Joan said with mock anger. "You are earning your keep. My servants are heavy-handed with the fabrics, but you are a careful worker. Besides, glad I am of your companionship. We'll find your brother yet. Now," she said as they entered the shop on the bridge, "we must get to work." Joan greeted a waiting customer, and Rose went into the storeroom.

Rose considered her situation. *'Twill not do, my staying here. One would have to be blind not to realize that Hugh is more than a servant to Joan. He'll soon be the master of the house, and when he is, he'll not want me around, especially when he finds out I'm with child. If I returned to Boxton, Cecily and Chris would surely take me in.* But the image of Seward Posthumous Potter, her graceless suitor, appeared in her mind, followed by the scorched patch of earth on the Green. "Nay, never," she declared, "I cannot go back."

Her back ached, and she had a throbbing pain in her head. She looked around for more barrels to unpack but found only two, the two that Joan had forbidden her to open. *Now, why should laces from East Friesland be so delicate that I cannot unpack them?* she wondered. *After all, Joan has just said I am a careful worker. Do the Frieslanders truly spin lace from gold?* A glance through the doorway into the shop told her that Joan was still occupied with the customer. She spied a crowbar lying on top of one of the barrels and slowly pried the lid off, stopping every time the wood creaked to check if Joan had heard her.

When she finally lifted the lid off the barrel, she was disappointed to find cards of ivory-colored lace which looked no different from some which she had unpacked on her first day of work. She dug her hands farther down into the barrel. "Paper! What on earth—" She pulled out a pamphlet. It was entitled *The Great Whore of Babylon.* She quickly scanned it and found it to be a scathing attack upon the Romish church. It was signed by someone who simply called himself "The Watchman." So Joan imported more than laces from East Friesland. She was a distributor of Protestant literature! Rose had heard talk of seditious writings being sent back to England by the exiles of Mary's reign. Had not the minister mentioned something about it in Saunders' barn that fateful day she had followed Derick to their meeting? This was more than heresy—this was treason!

Her heart beating wildly, she reached back into the barrel and found another pamphlet. This one was entitled *Jack-in-the-Box Mass,* apparently in derision of the pyx which held the wafer. Rose turned to the last page to see if it, too, was written by "The Watchman." She gasped when she saw the author's signature.

"Alas, I would not have taken you for a nosybody, Rose. You, spying into my private business." Joan had quietly entered the room, and as she spoke she closed the door behind her. "Put those papers back into the barrel, please—they are nothing but news from a foreign land."

Rose held up the pamphlet. Her eyes were bright with excitement, and her hand was trembling. "I know well enough what this is. I can read—and behold, this pamphlet, I think—nay, I *know*—was written by my brother, Robin!"

"Your brother? But how can you know that?"

"Here, here at the end," Rose leafed hurriedly back through the pages. She held the last page up for Joan. "See how it is signed?"

"Signed? Those are but a few pen scratches."

"Nay," Rose said triumphantly, "Those scratches are a bird track. 'Tis my brother's mark." She told Joan of their childhood games, with his mark a bird track and hers a rosebud. "Do you not see? My brother is with the exiles. He is printing for them. Did these truly come from East Friesland? Is the country far away?"

"Hush, hush, keep your voice down!" Joan whispered. "Aye, they do come from the town of Emden in East Friesland. 'Tis a small country the other side of the Netherlands on the North Sea. The rulers there are sympathetic to Protestant refugees."

"But my brother—how could he have paid for such a journey?"

"Wealthy believers paid the passage not only for young men who would train for the ministry, but also for printers and craftsmen to aid in their work."

"But can I be sure he's in Emden? Are there no exiles in other towns?"

"Oh, to be sure," Joan replied. "There are English congregations in Wesel, Basel, Frankfurt and Zurich, but 'tis in Emden that they print these pamphlets and send 'em to us. 'Tis a lovely city, Emden."

"You've been there? Then you might have seen my brother. Was there an Allworth, a few years older than I, with very light hair?"

"Whoa, girl," Joan laughed. "I sailed to Emden once as a messenger from the London congregation. I carried news of the martyrs and letters from friends and family of the exiles. I recall no name of Allworth on any of the messages—oh, but of course I might not have, since you are his only relative. Casting back in my mind, nay, I did not meet a man of that description. They all live in one large house. Stay you, I *do* recall that the few days I abode with them, the exiles mentioned that two of their number were away visiting the congregation in Wesel. If their names were told me, I remember not."

"If my brother is in Emden, I must know it. I can never rest until I find him."

"I am planning another trip to Emden soon." Joan smiled. "I confess the danger involved pleasures me. There are promoters abroad, you know, men commissioned by the Queen to seek out the more important exiles and bring them back to England for punishment. 'Tis good sport to outwit them and bring back messages right under their noses." She smoothed her gown. "Hugh accuses me of having a criminal mind, and I believe he's right."

"I could go in your place as messenger," Rose volunteered on impulse. *How else*, she told herself, *could she afford the passage to seek out her brother?* Joan had offered to pay her a small salary, but it would be months before she could save up enough to sail.

Joan considered for a moment. " 'Tis no venture lightly taken," she said solemnly. "One wrong move and you would endanger not only yourself but many others. I could go over and see if Robin is truly among the exiles. Then at a later time you could join him."

"Oh, I long to see him now." Rose did not mention that she was carrying a child, and so far Joan had not seemed to notice. "He's all the family I have, and I cannot describe the craving I have to see my own flesh and blood."

"Calm yourself, dear. We will speak more of this later. I cannot decide alone, in any wise."

As Rose became convinced that her brother was in Emden and not in London or any other part of England, the week seemed to drag by as she waited for Joan to agree to help her become the messenger. Each night she would lie in bed and imagine her reunion with her brother. Would he now be as wise and kind as their father had been? If he was wise, why had he chosen to flee to the Continent? Surely he was not a hot gospeller. Their father had never cared much for religion. His Great Bible had been more of a book of stories to him. Yet, Robin, like Derick, must have believed strongly to make such a change. Of course he had not laid down his life, but he had left his homeland. *Is my heart so cold,* she wondered, *that I cannot see what they see in their faith?*

On the Sabbath, Rose was awakened by Joan. "Get dressed quickly," she whispered. "The coventicle is meeting today, and I have permission to bring you. We must get their approval if you wish to act as messenger."

Rain had fallen that night and fog lay heavy over the bridge as they crossed into the city. They took a roundabout route even though their destination, Pudding Lane, was but a stone's throw from the bridge. The two women waited while Hugh entered a cobbler's shop and then returned after a few minutes, beckoning to them. They went through the shop and up narrow stairs into the living quarters above. Rose was surprised to see more than thirty people crowded into one room. Most of them watched her with the same expressions of distrust and fear that had been on the faces of the worshipers in Saunders' barn. A gentlewoman, whose cloak only partially concealed a richly brocaded gown, smiled at her and bowed to Rose. One man pressed through the tightly packed group and bowed to Rose. Joan introduced him as Deacon Olgrave.

"Good Sabbath, Widow Haler," he said cordially. "I had the privilege of seeing your husband as he and the others were led from Newgate to be taken to their own villages for execution. We welcome you to our congregation."

At the mention of Derick, Rose blinked back tears. She wanted to ask Deacon Olgrave if Derick had seemed frightened, if he had spoken at all, but she held her tongue. Everyone was still watching her. *If I could just talk again with someone from the village, I would say, "Remember how gentle he was with children?" and they would reply, "Aye, but could he not roar when he was angered!" I fear I shall forget his ways, his manner of speech,* Rose thought, *with no one to help me rehearse them.*

Everyone except the minister and the deacon, who acted as a guard at the door, sat down on the floor and waited for the service to begin. Rose let her mind turn back to Boxton. Perhaps she should have remained in the village. She might have found a good man to marry, one who would have provided safety and a home for her child, Emden. She had never even had a glimpse of the sea, and now she was offering to sail to a foreign land and carry messages. "Mother of Mercy, protect all fools, especially me," she prayed silently.

The deacon took roll while the minister, whom she had not yet met, was explaining Rose's presence to the people. Several turned around and looked at her with respect as the minister identified her as Derick's widow. "And now, let us spend a few moments in silent prayer for the families of the recent martyrs, the thirteen saints who endured the flames and went on to a better world on 27 June, at Stratford-le-bow."

Thirteen—and on the very day before I entered London, she thought. *By all that's holy, when will it stop?* She looked around at the heads bowed in prayer. *Can they all be insane, risking their lives as they do?* She caught the eye of a small boy who was peeking out between his fingers—*and the lives of their children?* Yet she could almost feel the love they had for one another. *Ah, well, perhaps Robin can teach me more of their faith when I reach Emden, if I am allowed to go.*

Following the sermon, Joan told the congregation of Rose's desire to replace her as messenger.

"I mean the Widow Haler no ill," said a sharp-faced man as he folded his arms in front of him, "but can a young widow from a small village be trusted with such a dangerous task? We know her rather little. What proof do we have of her sincerity?"

"Is not her husband's martyrdom proof enough?" Joan countered. "The very fact that she is unknown in London will be to our advantage. We can procure a false passport for her, and no one will be the wiser, whereas if I were to make another trip, I would be noticed no matter what name I traveled under, for I am of a rather unusual height."

"Rather!" exclaimed one young man, and he and the boy beside him both chuckled. The minister silenced them with a look.

"But, dear," the gentlewoman had turned to Rose, "are you willing to risk your life? If a promoter discovered that you aided the exiles, you could be arrested when you returned to England."

She considered before she replied. For some reason, Joan had chosen not to tell them that Rose planned to remain in Emden if her brother was there. In fact, she had not even mentioned the possibility of Robin being among the exiles. Perhaps it was because they might distrust someone with personal reasons for going abroad. "I want to do it," she said simply. "I have no home, no family here and no ties. I—" She groped for words. "I need to go. Please."

They asked her to wait downstairs while the congregation voted. She would be relieved if they turned her down. She was not certain that she was prepared to face another adventure. *Ah, well, 'tis out of my hands. The people upstairs said they desired God's will. Let them seek it, then.* She was tired of thinking about it.

At last she heard footsteps on the stairs. Joan descended with a broad smile on her face. "It has been decided. You will sail on the next ship to Emden."

Chapter Fourteen

JOAN BOOKED PASSAGE for Rose on a ship which would sail, weather permitting, the following Friday. "I go to meet with a maker of false passports this afternoon," she told Rose on Monday noon, "and I have made up a false address for you. Have you any preference for the name you'll be traveling under?"

Rose thought for a moment and then with a mischievous gleam in her eye said, "Terrel. Call me Widow Agnes Terrel." If there were to be any trouble on her journey, it would give her great satisfaction to involve the surname of the woman who had done such great harm to Derick.

On the evening before Rose was to sail, the women sewed packets of letters for the exiles into the petticoat she would wear on her journey. Joan stood by as her maid fit the petticoat and a new gown on Rose. After she had dismissed the maid Joan asked her, "I wist not you were with child. How far along be you?"

"About four months. The child is due in November."

"Such a tiny one, are you not? You hardly show at all. Why, when I was two months along, I looked as though I was carrying a melon."

"You have children?"

"Indeed I do," Joan replied proudly. "A son, sixteen years of age. I do not see him often. He lives with my brother in York. He's training to be a bladesmith. My son thinks that being a mercer is a womanly trade."

"You must miss him."

"Aye, but I'm glad he's in the North, away from all these troubles. Queen Mary casts not her shadow quite so far."

"Then your son is a believer?"

"Nay, but he is a youth, and a proper English youth at that and as hot-blooded as his mother. He'd have a hand in something dangerous here."

"I hope with all my heart I bear a son."

"God grant you do, dear," Joan gently replied. "And now you'd best get some sleep."

At dawn Joan accompanied her to the dock. Both women waited while Hugh carried her small trunk aboard. It contained several changes of clothing which Joan had given her. She also had insisted on sending enough money with Rose to buy her passage back to England if she failed to find her brother.

"The captain of this vessel is no Protestant, but he'll not trouble you. He swears he will have no other passengers, so if you keep to yourself and volunteer no information about the reason for your journey, there should be no danger. Now, have you memorized the address of the English house? And the password?"

"Aye, mother hen, you have asked me that three times," Rose answered with a laugh. "Fear not—I have burned them into my memory." She clasped Joan's hand. "And your generosity will ever linger in my heart. To befriend a stranger and treat her with such kindness—"

"Fie, 'tis nothing," Joan murmured, blushing at the compliment. "What is wealth for, if not to spend?" Hugh came down the gangplank and told Rose it was time for her to board. "Fare you well, Rose." Joan held her hand to her face to hide a tear. "You're a bold lass to be sure."

One of the crew led Rose below to a small cabin. "Am I the only passenger?" she asked him just to be sure.

"Aye, madam."

She breathed a sigh of relief. At least she would have no worry about a promoter on her voyage. The cabin was hot and stuffy, and she tried in vain to open the porthole. The seaman had told her she would have to stay below until the ship got underway, and she was not prepared for the constant motion of the vessel, even while it was moored. She began to feel dizzy and a little nauseous. "Oh, well," she said to herself, "if this is seasickness, 'tis nothing that can't be endured. After all, 'twill be but a two-day voyage."

As the ship traveled eastward on the Thames and out into the North Sea, however, she became so violently ill that she wished she could die. On the second day she managed to stagger on deck and was cheered by a glimpse of land in the distance. "At last!" she gasped, and asked one of the sailors when they would disembark.

He laughed. "That be the Netherlands, madam. We must sail beyond her to reach East Friesland."

When Emden was sighted at last, just the prospect of standing on firm ground helped her gain strength. In port she followed the crewman who carried her trunk down the gangplank, and then she was left to her own resources. As she looked around she saw a wagoneer leaning against his dappled horse. He smiled and touched his cap and ambled over to her. She repeated the address to the English House and held up a coin. He nodded and held up three fingers. Rehearsed in bartering by Joan, Rose frowned and held up two fingers, fearful all the while that he would refuse to drive her. He quickly agreed to the price and loaded her trunk onto his wagon.

As they traveled slowly through the town, Rose noticed that the streets were much cleaner than those of London. Most of the buildings were made of brick and had tiled roofs. Some of the women wore short-shouldered capes with collars turned up and embroidered white caps, similar to clothing worn in England. In a way she was disappointed, for she had expected foreigners to wear outlandish garb.

At last the driver stopped before the gate of a red brick house. *There must be some mistake,* she thought. *This place is as grand as Lord Endley's manor back home.* She recited the address again and the driver said, "Ja, ja," set her trunk down, and indicated that he would carry it to the door for another coin. After she had paid him she lifted the large brass doorknocker and took a deep breath before she let it fall against the door.

A severely dressed woman opened the door a few inches and without smiling said, "So?"

"Greetings from your sister in Smyrna." Rose's voice shook as she repeated the password which Joan had said was a reference to a persecuted church in the Book of Revelation. The woman continued staring at her, her head cocked to one side as if she were trying to understand. Rose repeated the message.

The woman nodded and smiled broadly. "Ah, die Engländerin," she said and closed the door in Rose's face, leaving her bewildered. She waited a while and was lifting the doorknocker again when the door opened. "Good-day, madam," said a young man. He was gazing at her with gray-green eyes, his straight eyebrows lifted in a quizzical expression as he waited for her to speak. His hair was almost snow white. Rose gasped and her eyes began to brim with tears.

The man looked perplexed. "The maid told me she thought you were English. Are you our sister from Smyrna?"

"Robin, oh, Robin, I *am* your sister. I'm Rose!"

"Rose? Can it truly be?" He stood back and studied her for a moment. "Aye, I see it now. My spindly baby sister has turned into a handsome woman." He hugged her, and she began to weep.

He handed her his kerchief. "Here now, no tears. This is a joyous occasion. Now tell me, how in the world did you find me?"

She started to answer but a man's voice called from inside the house, "Who is our visitor, Robin? Bring her in."

"In a moment," he replied and shut the door. "Come," he said as he led Rose through a side gate into the large garden behind the house. "We have much to discuss before I introduce you to the others." The garden was the fairest Rose had ever seen. There were rows and rows of flowers, some strange varieties which she had never seen. Trees shaded the stone benches along the paths, and in the farthest corner she could see a shady arbor whose vines bore scarlet flowers. She watched Robin as he dusted off a bench before they sat down. Now she noticed that his hairline was receding; he had a bit of a paunch, and fine lines were beginning to form around his eyes. *Soon he will look the image of our father,* she thought.

"Now," he was saying, "tell me all." She was hesitant at first, but soon she felt comfortable in his presence as she told him of her life after they had been separated, of her marriage to Derick, his death, of her journey to London, and finally of how she came to find his mark on the pamphlet.

"God has truly led you to me," he said when she had finished. He shook his head sadly. "I am so ashamed of myself. As the older, I should have been seeking you. At first, I did search for you diligently—I ran away from my master three times. Once I was past London's Wall, but he caught me. Then the old tyrant died and I was 'prenticed to a worthy man. 'Twas he who bought my passage to this place when Mary came to power. Things were better for me with my second master, and I pushed aside all thought of finding you. Forgive me."

"Oh, dear brother, there is nothing to forgive. My own desire to find you dimmed when I was wed. We were both young and had our own lives to live." She touched his arm. "What matters is that we are united again."

"But to think of you widowed and so ill-faring, and I was not there to aid you." He put his arm around her. "Be comforted, my little sister; I will take care of you now. And you will help us in our work, for you are an intelligent woman." He laughed, "You had to be—you are my sister. Now, when we . . .'"

As he talked on, Rose relaxed in the warmth of the sunshine on her back and the scent of flowers in the air. *I'm home at last,* she thought. *Robin is just as I had hoped he would be, kind and wise. I'll make myself useful and help him in his printing, and in the evening we will sit in this garden and have long talks about our childhood days. When the baby is born, Robin will be like a father to him—*

"Ro-BIN!" a shrill voice called. "Why are you hiding out there in the garden. Who is that with you?" A plump, raven-haired young woman, great with child, lumbered up to them. Robin had jumped up at her call and was holding out his hand to her.

"Mirabel!" he exclaimed, "you cannot surmise who our visitor—"

"That can wait," she interrupted and dismissed Rose with a glance. "Robbie, you must do something about that wretched cook. She shall never learn to make a proper English pudding."

Robin gave Rose an embarrassed grin and said quietly, "Rose, dear sister, I want you to meet Mirabel, my wife."

Chapter Fifteen

HOW STUPID OF ME, thought Rose. *I never once gave a thought to the fact that Robin might be married.* She smiled at Mirabel. "I am so pleased to meet you," she said as she extended her hand. Mirabel responded with a limp handshake and a weak smile.

After an awkward silence, Robin suggested they go inside. He led Rose into a large wood-paneled room that contained a printing press. At a long table, several men and four women were busily assembling pamphlets from printed quartos. They all looked up as Robin said, "Brothers and sisters, this is the messenger from the London congregation, Rose Haler, who also happens to be my sister in the flesh." They all rushed forward to meet her and besieged her with questions:

"What is the news from court?"

"Is it true that the Queen is deathly ill?"

"The Lady Elizabeth, is she safe and well?"

"What are the latest fashions in London?"

Rose was attempting to answer all of them when the floor seemed to start spinning beneath her. She had eaten nothing since early morning and was still weak from seasickness. Someone gripped her elbow and steadied her. "Fetch her a stool," a man's melodious voice ordered. The stool was brought, and when she was seated she looked up at the speaker. She reckoned him to be about thirty, and his face was quite comely in a lean, taut way. "Sister Beatrice," he was saying to a young woman, "verily, our visitor did not make such a perilous journey to advise you on fashions." His kind eyes belied the gentle mockery in his voice. He gave Rose a concerned appraisal and said, "Robin, I much admire your choice of kin."

Robin hastened to introduce him. "Rose, this is Thomas Stratton, a merchant from London whose generosity sustains us all."

"Fie, you make me sound like a pompous almsgiver! Any one of the brethren who had the means would do the same." He motioned for one of the women to get Rose something to drink and continued to stare at her until she blushed and looked away. A mug of cider was brought to her, and while she was drinking, another man said impatiently, "But what news do you bring us? Are there letters?"

"Aye," she assured him. She had almost forgotten the reason she had been sent to the exiles. "If I could have some scissors and a private place, I will loose the packets of letters sewn into my clothes."

The young woman, Beatrice, took her upstairs to a bedchamber and, once away from Thomas's hearing, deluged her with questions of fashions and court gossip. " 'Tis so dull here," she sighed. "My father is one of the ministers, and I have no social life. Most of my days are spent in this house with the same old people. Noah's daughters-in-law aboard the ark were no more shut in than I."

"But their lives were spared and so is yours," Rose replied with vigor. *Silly girl*, she thought, *has she forgotten the threat of death that brought her family to this haven in the first place?*

That evening as the exiles gathered in the great hall and read and re-read the letters she had brought, asking many questions about the London congregation which she could not answer, Rose caught Thomas Stratton watching her several times. After prayers, Pastor Bradbury, Beatrice's father, said, "Widow Haler, Robin tells me that you wish to remain with us for a time. We welcome you into our fellowship.—Beatrice, you and the other unmarried girls must make room for her in your bedchamber.—And now, brethren, shall we to bed?"

As Rose followed Beatrice up the stairs, Thomas Stratton brushed past her and then turned and put his hand on the railing, blocking her way.

"Widow Haler," he began.

"Rose, if you please."

"Rose," he said smiling at her. "Rose—aye, it fits you well." He cleared his throat. "I just want to add my personal welcome."

"Why, thank you, Master Stratton."

"Thomas, if you please." He mimicked her with a twinkle in his eye. "Well—I—welcome, again." He turned and bounded up the stairs.

Although Rose had to share a feather bed with Beatrice, she was grateful to be lying on a mattress that did not toss with every wave of the sea. Amid roommates' whispered conversations she tried to sort out her thoughts. This had not been the reunion with Robin she had anticipated—and yet, she reflected ruefully, what *had* come about as she had imagined it since the first she left Boxton? Robin seemed a worthy man—a bit soft, perhaps. As for his wife Mirabel—well, she would try to love her as a sister. And Thomas Stratton—she blushed to think of him—for a gentleman he had such manliness, and his voice was so pleasant to the ear . . . She drifted off to sleep.

As the weeks passed and summer turned to autumn, Rose tried to fit into the routine of the English House. She soon sorted out the different relationships among the exiles. Besides the parents of Beatrice and the other two girls who were sisters, there were three young married pairs with five small children among them; Robin and Mirabel, expecting their first child; one youth about sixteen who was Robin's apprentice; and another minister who, with Beatrice's father, acted as shepherd of the flock and trained several of the young married men for the ministry. Thomas was a widower: she was surprised how much it pleased her to learn that.

In fact, the more she learned about him, the more she liked him. Although he paid for everyone's food and for the hire of the servants, he never lorded it over the others but placed himself under the authority of the ministers. In the nightly theological discussions the men enjoyed, he spoke little, but when he did, the others listened. Thomas was in charge of purchasing supplies and keeping in contact with the other English congregations on the Continent, so he was often away for days at a time. Rose found herself missing his presence more each time he left, although they had exchanged but a few words, and those in the presence of others.

For the women, the highlight of the day seemed to be their trip to market, accompanied by Hansi, the one maidservant who knew some English. Despite having her as translator, it was difficult to buy the ingredients for dishes they were accustomed to serve in England. At first Rose thought it would be much easier for the women to let the cook prepare the local specialties, but after a few weeks she too began to long for some good English ale and a wedge of Essex cheese.

After market, the women would care for their own families' needs, and in the time left they helped assemble pamphlets. Rose enjoyed that most of all. Robin delighted in teaching her how the press worked—Mirabel had never been interested, he said. After a while, Robin gave Rose the choice task of proofreading manuscripts, and she worked long hours beside her brother.

Mirabel seemed to grow increasingly jealous of every moment Robin spent with Rose. Matters came to a head one afternoon in September when Rose had gently pointed out to Mirabel that she had sewn the pages of a pamphlet together in the wrong order.

"How dare you criticize me!" Mirabel cried as she threw down the pamphlet and flounced off to her bedchamber.

Robin followed her and later told Rose, "Mayhap you could show more kindness to my wife, sister. She is tender-eared and thinks you somewhat overcritical of her."

Bright red splotches appeared on Rose's neck as she fought to keep her temper. *Overcritical, indeed!*

Robin tentatively took her hand and said, "I had hoped you two would become fast friends, and when Mirabel's time comes you could be her nurse."

I'd sooner be an adder's nurse, Rose thought, but forced herself to speak sweetly. "Robin, can you not see? I carry a child also. Mirabel will deliver before I shall, but one of the unmarried girls would make a better nurse. Let them wash her baby's napkins and be at her beck and call."

He looked puzzled. "Oh, but of course! I cannot think why Mirabel would expect you to wait upon her in those circumstances."

He looked so distressed that she kissed him on the cheek. "I shall try to get along with your wife, dear brother," and then she playfully patted his balding head. "I don't want you to lose any more of your lovely hair by worrying."

After dinner one evening, when the young children had been tucked into bed, the women sat in a circle and sewed while the men discussed Scripture. For an hour the women had been talking of their life "back home" and longing for the sturdy English woolens, the fairs, and the seamstresses they had employed who could fit a gown to perfection. Rose became bored and strained to hear the men. The two who were being trained for the ministry seemed to be having an argument over some minor point.

"Erasmus clearly stated in his translation—" began one.

"If you will but look in the original Greek—" interrupted the other.

"Stop!" Rose stood up so quickly her stool fell over. "How can you sit here in safety and babble over some detail when your own brethren are dying in England? If God cares so little what happens to His followers, do you think He bothers one whit about whatever you are debating?" She paused for breath and, seeing the shock on all their faces, ran out into the garden, slumped down on a bench and covered her burning face. She rocked back and forth as she cried bitterly, "No one cares, no one cares."

"I care." She looked up and saw Thomas standing in front of her. "And God cares," he continued as he sat down beside her. "God cares about Rose Haler and her grief and loneliness—and He loves her." She looked away from him, but he touched her cheek and turned her face back toward his own, gently wiping away her tears with his handkerchief. "Robin has told me of the manner of your husband's death. I'm sorry. My wife died several years ago after a long illness."

"But that was a natural death," she burst out. "Derick as much as killed himself by professing his belief."

He was silent for a moment and then he said softly, "You are not a true believer, are you?" It was not a question.

The words seemed to slap Rose in the face. She had tried to enter into the exiles' worship services as a matter of courtesy, but she had not realized that her lack of personal belief was so obvious. "Nay, I am not," she whispered.

"You do but state what God already knows," he told her.

"I want to believe," she said haltingly, "but one man says this, another that, and men are burned and—" Warmed by his comforting presence, Rose began to weep again.

He put his arm around her and waited until she had finished, then said earnestly, "Look not upon us men, poor creatures that we are. Look to Christ. Listen to His voice. Our heavenly Father is waiting to give you life more abundant. The Scriptures say that there is not one who has left family or houses or lands to serve God that He will not restore to them what they have left, and more."

"You are so kind. I'm sorry I slandered you all. 'Tis just—why do some have to die so horribly and others remain free?"

"I know not all the answers, I know only why I became one of the self-banished when Mary came to power. I felt God could use me more, use my abundant means, to preserve a remnant of the faithful believers. The Queen will not live forever; some day, God willing, Elizabeth will come to power and abolish popery. Then we shall return with our newly trained young ministers and laymen and help our people back to the true ways. Now, back to your own beliefs, Rose—"

She suddenly realized that his arm had been around her shoulder all this time and jumped up. "Thank you. I've made such a fool—good-night." She hurried off to bed.

Chapter Sixteen

THE NEXT MORNING Rose lingered in the bedchamber after everyone else had gone down to breakfast. She was ashamed of her angry outburst the night before, and she dreaded facing the others, especially Thomas. To think that she cried on the shoulder of another man. *'Twas shameful,* she thought. She barely knew him. Still, last night in the garden she felt she had known him for a long time.

An hour passed and she grew restless. *Very well,* she decided. *I have faced more dreaded times than this. I shall go down and be done with it. If I must face each person singly and beg his forgiveness, I shall do it most humbly and*—there was a knock on the door. *Here's my first pardoner.* She took a deep breath and said, "Come in."

Her face fell as Mirabel entered, accompanied by Hansi the maidservant. *Merciful saints, must she be the first?* she swallowed hard and then sputtered out, "Forgive me for last night—"

"Rose, dear, could you do a service for the congregation?" Mirabel had plowed right over her apology.

"Why, certainly," Rose answered, taken aback by Mirabel's pleasant attitude.

"We wedded women are so busy caring for our own *husbands*"— she emphasized the word—"and the children that we cannot go to market today, and if we send the three foolish virgins who share this room with you, they would surely bring home moldy cheeses and rotted fruits. Would you take Hansi and go to market alone?"

"I would be joyed to do so." Rose was relieved that Mirabel had not gloated over her apology. She was pleased to be able to do a favor for the congregation. What better way to show she was truly penitent? "What shall I buy?" she asked eagerly.

"Oh, I have written a list. 'Tis in this purse with the coins. You need not bother looking at it now." Mirabel smiled as she handed the purse to her, and for a moment she reminded Rose of a cat that had just swallowed a mouse.

I'll not mistrust her. Perhaps she truly desires to be my friend, Rose thought.

"Hansi, take Madam down the backstairs. 'Twill be faster."

Rose and the maidservant met no one as they went out the back door and through the garden. As they walked into the center of Emden, without the insulation of other English women beside her, Rose felt again as if she were a true sojourner in a distant land. 'Twas a strange feeling not to be able to read signs or understand the bits of conversation she heard from bystanders along the streets.

When they arrived at the market square, Rose opened the purse Mirabel had given her and took out the marketing list. *What a careless thing to do!* she thought. *Mirabel has written the list on a page torn from one of the pamphlets which we labored so long to assemble. Robin would be in a rage if he knew.* She turned the page over and saw that it contained a very harsh denouncement of Queen Mary. *I could return this page to her in Robin's presence. Wouldn't there be a fine row!— Nay, she was kind to me today, I'll not stir up trouble.* She sighed and said, "Hansi, let us begin with chickens. Now we want no aged hens but nice, plump—" She felt a hand on her shoulder.

"What are you doing here?"

"Oh, Master Stratton, Thomas, you startled me."

He grabbed her arm and looked around quickly. "All of the women were ordered to stay inside today," he whispered. "Surely someone must have informed you. I was looking for you when one of the children told me she saw you leave with Hansi, carrying a marketing basket."

"I knew not—but what is wrong?" She had never seen him upset before.

"An Englishman was seen in the town. He was asking questions about the English House." He lowered his voice. "I'll wager he's a promoter."

"But Mirabel told me to do the marketing."

"She knew of the danger, for she was sitting across from me at breakfast when I made the announcement. What is this?" He took the pamphlet page from her. "If you had been captured with this on your person and the promoter had smuggled you aboard a ship to England, you would have been executed for treason." He turned to

Hansi who had been trying in vain to follow their conversation. "Hansi, no marketing today. Go visit your mama. I shall take Madam home."

As they walked rapidly away from market, Rose thought about Mirabel. Had she sent her out marketing merely to get her into more trouble with the congregation by disobeying orders, or had she actually hoped that Rose would be captured by the promoter? Surely the use of the pamphlet page signified the latter. Robin had told her that he had wed Mirabel shortly after the exiles had arrived in Emden two years ago. Her father had fallen overboard and drowned on the voyage over, and she was left an orphan. Poor Robin! For a marriage vow made out of kindness he had bought himself a lifetime of misery. Not that he realized it yet. Mayhap this incident would open his eyes.

Thomas led her in a roundabout route, making sure they were not followed, and took her through the back entrance. "You'll be safe within these grounds," he said. "The congregation is under the protection of the Duchess of Oldenburg. If there is a promoter about, he cannot openly storm the house. He'll likely hire local villains and try to spirit one of us away."

" 'Twould be you they would covet to capture," she said worriedly.

"They'll have little chance. I leave today for Frankfurt."

"But, Thomas, why?" He and Robin were the only ones who made her life bearable.

"I was seeking you this morning to tell you. I received a letter from my friend, Richard Chambers. In addition to their arguments over doctrine and pastoral authority, some in the Frankfurt congregation are accusing Chambers of wrongly using the funds he collected from London merchants. I must go to his defense." He hesitated a moment, then taking her hands, led her behind the arbor where they were hidden from view of the house. "When I return, I shall have something of importance to say to you." He paused and looked deeply into her eyes. "Nay, I must say it now. From the moment I first saw you, I've admired your courage and your honesty—and you must know you are quite comely to look upon."

"Even in my mothering state?" she asked without thinking, then blushed.

"Especially so, since you are performing a woman's holiest duty, the giving of life. Today as I searched the town for you, fearing that you might have been captured, I—well, I realized that I not only admire you—I love you." He bent his head down and kissed her softly on the lips. The kiss was over before she had time to resist, but his touch made her heart beat so wildly that she hardly heard his next words:

"Rose, dearling, will you be my wife?"

She was speechless, and he plunged on, "I know this is of a sudden, but it is not improper. The Scriptures plainly say that when one of a wedded pair has died, the other may seek another mate. I have been so lonely these past two years and I wist that you are lonely, too. I would vow to be a goodly father to your child, I—I cannot say fitting words." He held her tightly to him and in his embrace she felt protected and cherished. He kissed her once more and as a flood of longing swept over her, she returned his kiss with fervor. Suddenly Derick's face flashed before her eyes, and she pulled away from Thomas in horror.

Rose stood trembling as Thomas searched her eyes for the reason for her sudden resistance. "I was too hasty in my affection. Forgive me," he said. "Nay, speak not," he pleaded as she opened her mouth. "We will speak further when I return in a fortnight. In the meanwhile I shall pray God will settle your heart and grant you the grace to trust Him. Farewell," he said softly, "Farewell, my heart's desire." Then he disappeared through the gate.

Rose's lips were still aflame with his last kiss, and she rubbed them with the back of her hand and cried, "Oh, Derick, I've betrayed your memory! But oh, my dearest, I am so lonely! What would you have me do?"

Blinded by tears, she hurried up the backstairs to her bedchamber. In the hallway she bumped into Mirabel as she was carrying a pile of linen. "Have a care!" Mirabel cried.

"Oh, 'tis you. Did you purchase everything on the list?"

Rose hurled the purse at her face and brushed past her. As she reached her bedchamber, she turned and called angrily, "Your time shall come, Mirabel!"

Chapter Seventeen

BUT MIRABEL HAD the good sense not to be caught alone with Rose during the next few days. As for Rose, she was in such turmoil over Thomas's proposal and her own alarming reaction to it that she scarcely gave another thought to Mirabel's trickery. She kept to herself and spent her evenings strolling in the garden.

One night as she stood on the very spot where Thomas had kissed her, she argued with herself. *'Twas shameful to return his kiss—but 'twas honorably given. He wants me to be his wife— Derick has been dead but a few months, but I am alive and so lonely. Oh, what to do, what to do? Thomas shall return in ten days' time, and what answer shall I give him?* The evening was beginning to get chilly. She decided to join the others in the great hall. *Mayhap I've over-wearied my mind on this matter. Some simple conversation would be good. After all, I do have over a week to decide before he returns.*

Everyone was in his customary place. The men were in a circle, listening to Pastor Bradbury. The women were near the light of the fireplace, mending or reading. Except for Mirabel. She was lodged in the most comfortable chair, with her feet, very swollen from pregnancy, propped up on cushions. Robin looked up as Rose entered.

"And who is this stranger?" he teased. "What fair damsel is this who graces us with her presence?"

Rose smiled weakly and sat down on a cushion.

"As I was saying," Pastor Bradbury, Beatrice's father, was speaking, "there has been no further threat of a promoter in Emden." He had raised his voice to include all the women in this announcement. "This afternoon when I made inquiries around the town, there was no sign of another Englishman. One mariner said that there was indeed one who landed last week, but I think we can

104

assume that he was a harmless traveler who was but passing through."

"Father, may we go marketing tomorrow, then?" Beatrice asked him eagerly.

Bradbury looked at the other men who nodded. "Very well. I see no harm in it."

"I'll not be able to," Mirabel whined, "with these poor swollen limbs.—Robin, fetch me a pillow for my back." He brought her a cushion from the floor. "Not that hard thing—I want my down pillow from the bedchamber." He hurried off to get it.

"Here it is, my dove, let me put it behind your back—"

Mirabel pushed it away. "I want it no longer, Robbie. What I long for is a bit of cider."

"Stay." Rose told her brother as she arose, "I shall fetch it for her. I want one myself." She could not bear to see her brother ordered about like a trained dog. She went to the kitchen and took a long swallow of cider and then poured one out for Mirabel.

"Here you are, Mirabel," she said, forcing a smile as she handed her a mug.

"Ugh, I can't drink out of that awful mug!—Robbie, I want my silver cup." She shoved the mug back into Rose's hand, splashing some of the cider onto Rose's skirt. Rose shoved back and the mug fell into Mirabel's lap. She gasped and awkwardly leaped to her feet.

"You did that on purpose, you wicked woman!" she shouted at Rose, shaking her fist in Rose's face. Rose pushed her back into the chair.

"Me wicked—*me*? Why, you—" Rose let loose a stream of the worst kind of oaths, words Derick had often used before he was converted. They shocked even Rose as she said them, but she could not stop herself. When she finished there was dead silence in the room.

Mirabel said loudly, with a triumphant smile on her face, "There, 'tis proof! She's but a false professor—she belongs not here with us."

Trembling, Rose looked down at Mirabel and said calmly, "For once you have spoken the truth. I do not belong here." She knew now what she must do. She still had the money Joan had given her for a return voyage. She would leave Emden before Thomas returned. She was uncertain that she would be firm in her resolve if he were here.

She was gathering up her things in the bedchamber when Robin entered.

"Sister, take not Mirabel's words to heart. We all—'tis difficult to live in harmony in such close quarters. As for the cursing, everyone forgets St. James' admonitions about the tongue at one time or another." His wide brow was wrinkled with concern.

"Mirabel will never like me."

"When the child is born she'll feel better and—"

"Nay, she deliberately provoked me tonight, and I could tell you—ah well, let it be. Robin, I wish to return to England."

"But we've just become reacquainted—I'll speak sternly to Mirabel."

" 'Tis not just Mirabel. I have other reasons." She thought of Thomas. "The one I cannot tell you, and the other—'tis as Mirabel said, I am no true believer. I do not belong here."

"But in time, when you're more settled in your widowed state—"

"Mayhap, but not in this place."

"But you belong here with me."

He looked so crestfallen that Rose went over and kissed him on the cheek. "Dear brother, I know not where I belong. I have become quite a wanderer these few months past, but I know now that I must go back to London. I'm certain Joan will let me stay with her until my baby is born. Wherever I go will be an imposition on someone, but I'd sooner it be in London than in this small bit of England in a foreign land." She looked up into his face, at the same high forehead and straight eyebrows she and her father had. "We are family and will always be, whether we ever meet again or not. But you have your place and I—I must find mine."

After a while Robin realized that any further argument was futile. "You have inherited the family stubbornness, I see," he wryly observed. She persuaded him to take her money and buy her passage on the next ship sailing for England. Mirabel did not hide her satisfaction when she learned Rose was leaving, but the others seemed genuinely sorry to see her go.

On the morning of her departure, Beatrice took her aside. "I'm grieved that you are leaving. I shall miss you."

"I shall miss you also, Beatrice," Rose said and meant it, for the girl was the only female of the congregation she felt at home with. *Such a pleasant girl,* she thought. *Comely, too, with those big brown eyes.* Rose felt a stab of jealousy as she realized that after she left, Thomas might choose Beatrice to be his wife.

"Would you do me a kindness?" Beatrice was saying. "I have a dear friend in London—we were children together. Would you take my letter to her?"

Rose hesitated. Robin had insisted that she carry no messages or pamphlets back with her for safety's sake, yet—one letter to a young girl—

"Aye, I shall take it."

She placed the letter under her clothing in the trunk. "Farewell, Beatrice. Oh, and when Thomas Stratton returns, will you tell him—"

"Yes?"

What can I say, Rose thought—*that if and when I feel free to love someone, it could be he? What consolation would that be to a lonely man?* "Just tell him," she said aloud, "that I wish him well."

Only after she had told Robin good-bye and was walking up the gangplank did she give a thought to the problem that had beset her on her voyage over. She looked down at the water splashing between the ship and the dock and dizziness swept over her. "Mother of Mercy, not seasickness again." She paused halfway between the ship and shore; then Mirabel's whining voice echoed in her mind *"Robbie, Robbie."* "Better this than that," she muttered and in two quick steps she was on board.

Chapter Eighteen

"WELCOME ABOARD, Widow Terrel."

Rose was taken aback to hear herself again called by that distasteful name, but she recovered in time to give the first mate a smile as she followed him below to her cabin. As a further precaution, Robin had decided that she should again travel under the name of her false passport. No one had even asked to see it on her trip over, but it might be a different matter when she disembarked in London. This was a larger ship than the one that had brought her over to Emden, and as it set sail she was pleased to discover that she was not at all seasick this time. That evening when the cabin boy brought an invitation from the captain for her to join him for dinner, she readily accepted.

The captain and first mate were already seated when she joined them. Captain Peterssen was a Scandinavian, Robin had said, and Rose was relieved to find that he spoke almost perfect English. "Ah, madam," he said as he rose to his feet, "we are glad you consented to dine with us. Please take a seat." He was a large, florid man with a reddish-gold beard that billowed out from his chin.

The cabin boy began to serve them, but the captain held up his hand. "We will wait for our other guest." He turned to the first mate. "I wonder what is keeping our other passenger?"

"Other passenger?" Rose asked as her heart began to beat rapidly. "I saw no one else come aboard."

"So comical it was," said the first mate, watching the doorway as he spoke. "At the last moment, this Englisher wanted to buy passage for himself and his master. I told him the wind would wait for no man, but if they could come aboard before we cast off, well and good. After you, madam, were in your cabin and we were about to get underway, here this one comes running with his master huffing and puffing behind him. The servant was carrying a trunk on his shoulder and he slipped going up the gangplank. The trunk fell into the sea and he almost went with it. His master was in a rage and kicked—" he broke off as a man entered.

"Ah, here you are," said the captain, a little too cordially. "Widow Terrel, may I present Master Habishaw. Since you are both from England, I am sure you will have much pleasant conversation."

"Delighted," Habishaw murmured and bowed. She thought his face looked as if nature had formed perfect features and then in a fit of whimsy had stretched them out of proportion. His nose and chin were a bit too long, his mouth too wide and thin. As he sat down across from her and fastidiously wiped his knife and spoon with his napkin, she saw that even his fingers were narrow and overlong.

As food was passed, Habishaw tried to engage Rose in conversation, but Captain Peterssen, busily attacking a roasted chicken, motioned for silence. Apparently he thought talk and food did not mix. She was grateful for the time to collect her thoughts. She had been taken off guard, she knew, and if this Habishaw were a promoter, one hastily spoken word could endanger Joan and the other members of the London congregation.

At last the captain arranged the chicken bones in a neat pile on his plate, pushed back his chair and, when he had ordered more wine poured all around, said, "Well, now, tell us about yourself, Habishaw. What business had you in Emden?"

Habishaw didn't answer immediately. He ran one slender finger around the edge of his cup and then slowly replied, "Oh, you might call me a seeker of treasure." He watched Rose as he spoke. "I find—items—that would be of use to Her Majesty, the Queen, and bring them back to her."

"Then you've had little luck in Emden, I'll wager," the captain said with a laugh. For some reason Habishaw turned red and clenched his fists. Captain Peterssen continued, "The New World— now that's where treasure's to be found. I've heard tales of cities of gold and mountains of silver. Why, a Spaniard told me—" He launched into a long story while Rose nervously crumpled her napkin into a ball under Habishaw's steady scrutiny.

"And you, madam, why have you gone abroad?" Habishaw suddenly asked while the captain was pausing for breath.

She had her answer ready. "My husband died of most grievous injuries when his horse threw him. I could not ease my sorrow and so I thought a sea journey would calm my tormented mind." Her voice quivered as she spoke.

"To Emden and back, unaccompanied, in your condition? Surely that was not a wise undertaking. Have you acquaintances in Emden?" His eyes narrowed as he waited for her reply.

"I—" she felt as if a weight were pressing down on her chest. As she was groping for words she caught the captain's eye. "Please—" she began.

"You are seasick, no?" he said, coming to her aid.

She nodded weakly.

"Lief," he ordered the first mate, "escort the lady to her cabin."

"If I may," said Habishaw, coming around to her chair.

"Nay, you remain," Peterssen commanded. "I want to hear more about your treasure hunting."

"You remain also," Rose told the first mate. "I can manage alone.—Thanks to you for the dinner," she told the captain. *And for the excuse to leave,* she thought.

Once outside the room she dreaded going into her own cramped quarters and decided to slip up on deck for a few breaths of fresh air. Peterssen would no doubt use Habishaw as an unwilling audience for his sea stories for some time. As she put her foot on the first step, she heard voices above and paused to wait until the speakers had passed.

"Avast, who goes there?" She heard one call out.

" 'Tis Evans, Master Habishaw's servant."

"Ah, you be the one what dropped a trunk in the briny." The voice laughed. "I seen your master kick you across the deck."

"He's a mean one to be sure," growled Evans. "He's coming home empty-handed and taking it out on me."

"Empty-handed of what?"

"He's a promoter. You know, he catches heretics. They sent him over to fetch back a rich one; but just before my master lays hands on him, he ups and escapes to Frankfurt. We followed him a ways but lost him."

Rose stifled a cry. *Thomas! They had nearly captured Thomas!* She hurried to her cabin and bolted the door. She sat on her bunk and tried to stop trembling. Thomas could have been aboard this very ship, as a prisoner of Habishaw on his way to his death! She thought of the way he had looked at her as he had declared his love, of his kiss. *Oh, I was a fool to leave Emden: Why am I forever running from safety into loneliness and danger? Surely in time, as Derick's memory faded, I would have come to love him. But could I have endured the stifling closeness of the English House and Mirabel?* She thought back to the time—was it only thirteen months ago?—when her only complaint was the constant rain, her only enemy was mildew. "Oh, God above," she cried bitterly, "will I never have a home again?"

For the rest of the voyage, she kept to her cabin, pleading seasickness. She was famished eating just the biscuits and flat ale the captain had sent to settle her stomach. But if she kept out of Habishaw's way, she reasoned, she would be safe. She was grateful to Robin for not allowing her to carry any pamphlets back to England. Once they had landed, she could slip through the throng, and when she had made sure she wasn't followed, return to Joan's house on the bridge.

When it was time to disembark she gave Habishaw plenty of time to leave the ship before she opened her cabin door. Finally she opened it slightly, and a man's boot stepped into the opening.

"Good-day, madam." Habishaw and his servant had been standing in front of the door and now prevented her closing it. "I see you have fully recovered from seasickness. Evans, carry the lady's trunk." Habishaw took her firmly by the elbow and escorted her above deck. She looked about for the captain, but he must have been below supervising the unloading of cargo.

Once they were ashore, Rose saw Habishaw give his servant a nod and Evans deliberately dropped the trunk from his shoulder. It landed upside down and the lid flew open, spilling her clothing on the ground.

"Evans, you clumsy idiot, look what you've done," Habishaw mildly exclaimed.

As Rose stooped down to pick up her belongings, she tried to keep her temper. *A man with Habishaw's influence could easily have me arrested for the slightest reason. At least he would find no mess—Beatrice's letter!* It had fallen into the mud a few feet away from the trunk. Just as she reached for it, Habishaw's hand darted past her and retrieved the letter.

"Give it to me," she demanded, holding out her hand, but Habishaw held it out of her reach as he tore it open.

He quickly read through it and said with an icy smile. "This is most interesting. 'Tis signed by a Beatrice Bradbury—Bradbury, that is the name of a heretical preacher who escaped to Emden in 1554. Look you, Evans," he said, " 'twas not a fruitless journey after all. We have apprehended one of the heretic's messengers. Here, take her other arm. We'll escort Widow Terrel to her lodgings."

Chapter Nineteen

ROSE WAS NUMB with fear as the two men propelled her along the lane and across London Bridge to the Southwark side, to the prison known as the Clink. When they passed Joan's shop on the bridge, she looked around frantically, hoping someone would spot her and tell Joan, but the door to the shop was closed, and she saw no one who would recognize her. Habishaw and his servant took her to the wardroom of the prison, and when an undersheriff had been summoned, Habishaw began his preliminary interrogation.

"Now, then, Widow Terrel," he began.

"Haler," she corrected him in a voice that was barely a whisper.

"What? Speak up," he commanded.

"My name is Rose Haler."

"No matter the name you wish to use, you were caught carrying seditious messages from heretics."

Anger brought the blood racing back to her head, and she spoke in a louder tone. "I merely carried a harmless letter from a young girl to her friend."

" 'Twas written by a heretic, was it not?"

"I—"

" '—and when Bloody Mary is taken from the throne, we can return home from exile,' " Habishaw quoted. He turned to the undersheriff. "There is more, sir." He pointed to a line of the letter. "Here begins a mockery of His Holiness, the Pope."

Oh, Beatrice, if you but knew the harm you have done me, thought Rose. Aloud she said, "I wist not the contents of the letter." She began to feel the floor moving under her feet.

"A likely story. Now to other matters. What are the names of the members of the London congregation?"

Everything went black, and as Rose fell to the floor, she heard

Habishaw say, " 'Tis but trickery to avoid examination."

"I have a remedy for that," said the undersheriff. "We'll convey her to the cage. A day spent as a gazingstock will loosen her tongue." Rose lost consciousness completely.

"Traitor!"

"Whore!"

"Heretic!"

When Rose awoke she was half-sitting, half-lying down in a wooden box about four feet wide by four feet deep. There were bars across the front which separated her from those who were mocking her. She drew back as a little boy poked a stick through the bars. "Get her, Jamie boy, get her," urged the child's mother. Rose got to her feet just as an old crone spit at her.

"Oh, look, the whore is carrying a whelp. Soon they can burn you both at the same time."

The guard shoved the woman away with his stick. "Go on with you, old mother, you're blocking the way. There's gentlefolk want to pass by."

Rose pressed her face against the bars and peered sideways. The cage was at the entrance to London Bridge! She turned from the curious stares and then reeled back when she heard:

"Oh, God have mercy!" It was Joan, standing before the cage with a horrified expression on her face. "Rose, what has befallen you?" She grasped her hand through the bars. "Oh, Hugh, come and see," she called to her steward. "We must do something. Oh, poor dear.—Release her!" she ordered the guard.

"That I cannot do, madam," he answered. "I am to keep her here until sundown and return her to the keeper at the Clink."

Rose had begun to cry at the sight of her friend. As sobs wracked her body, she clung to Joan's hand as a drowning man would cling to a rope.

"Look at her flushed face! She's dying of thirst! Give her to drink," Joan bellowed to the guard.

"If she's thirsty, I've a lovely drink for the heretic." The old crone was back and was carrying a chamber pot. She swung it back. "Here, dearie, just what you—augh!"

Joan had wrested the pot from her. "Drink your own brew, witch!" she roared as she dumped the pot over the old woman's head.

The guard stepped between the two. "Here you," he said to Joan, "gentry or no, you can't be disturbing the peace. Away with you, or I'll call a constable."

Hugh stepped between Joan and the guard. "My mistress meant no harm," he said in a soothing voice. "Come, madam," he pleaded as the guard backed off. "You cannot help her if you, too, are arrested."

"Take heart, Rose. I'll go to the authorities. We'll have you released in no time."

Now Rose was again left to the mercy of the rabble. She tried to cover her ears to shut out the vile names they called her, but she still heard their taunts. "Heretic, why doesn't your God rescue you?" one man shouted.

Why indeed, she thought. *God, I've done no wrong. An act of kindness turned to my harm. Haven't you done enough to me? You've taken my husband; will you also kill me and the child?* "If you can hear me, release me!" she prayed. She had a vague remembrance of reading in the Bible where prison doors had miraculously opened when St. Paul was imprisoned. "Very well," she told God, "if Beatrice and the rest are your true believers and I have been arrested for aiding them, then come to my defense. Cause this door to open." She waited, but when nothing happened, she began to giggle hysterically. "Fool," she told herself. "Did you expect He would answer you, that He would send a lightning bolt to strike the door and burst it open?" She clutched the bars in her anguish, and someone spit in her face.

Somehow sunset came at last. She had hoped to the final moment that Joan would return with an order for her release, but there was no sign of her as Rose was taken back across the bridge to the Clink. After the door to her cell had been shut, the overwhelming stench of the filthy straw on the floor caused her to gag and retch. In the darkenss, she felt around with her foot until she touched the rough canvas pallet that was to be her bed. Her bones ached, and she felt a terrible gnawing in her belly, for she had been given nothing to eat or drink since the biscuits and ale of the day before. She collapsed on the pallet, but when she heard scurrying sounds by her head, she quickly got to her feet. *It must be rats,* she thought. *If she fell asleep, they might gnaw at her fingertips or her nose.* She shuddered and tried to rest standing up, leaning against the moldy wall. The weight of the child she carried pressed heavily upon her and sent shooting pains down her legs. When she closed her eyes, she saw the hateful faces that had taunted her through the bars of the cage.

"Why, Why?" she cried out in her misery. "I did no wrong—I was blameless—I—" In that instant she saw in her mind how Christ must have looked as He hung on the cross. He had been scourged, mocked, and forced to carry His own cross, she remembered. He had been tortured with nails driven through His hands and feet, and then hung in agony, a gazingstock before an angry multitude. But He was the innocent Son of God, the only begotten of His Father. What had He said of His life? "No man taketh it from me, but I lay it down of myself." [1] She let her mind dwell on His holiness. Compared to the hateful people who had hurled abuse at her and the horrible creature who spit in her face, even compared to the real Widow Terrel, she was positively saintly. But oh, compared to that innocent One who died such a death! She remembered the words of John the Baptist, "Behold the Lamb of God, which taketh away the sin of the world." [2]

Measured against the sinlessness of Christ, she saw her own heart, as black and filthy as her cell. The realization of her self-centered life—to think she hadn't wanted Derick's new-found faith to shatter her safe existence—her impatience and lack of sympathy for the exiles. And yes, even Mirabel—had she been any kinder to Mirabel? All these sins and a thousand more flashed before her mind and under the searching light of God's purity. She dropped to her knees and cried aloud, "Forgive me, oh, forgive me!"

"For the wages of sin is death, but the gift of God is eternal life through Jesus Christ our Lord." [3] The verse came to her mind as clearly as if someone had spoken it. Suddenly she knew, she really knew why Christ had allowed himself to be crucified. "He died for me. He died for *me!*" He had borne *her* sins on the cross, had endured *her* punishment. She tried to pray but could only repeat over and over, "Thank you, Lord Jesus, thank you." The prison door had not swung open, but something more miraculous had occurred: her sins had been forgiven. She felt Christ's presence with her, strengthening her, loving her. With a long shuddering sigh of relief, she lay down on the pallet and immediately fell asleep.

At dawn a shaft of light from a grating high up in the wall fell across her face. She stirred and felt something brush against her leg. She sat up in time to see a rat slip through a small hole in the corner of the cell. She gingerly stood up. At least she had not been bitten! Her head was pounding. There was a clanking sound at the door and someone thrust a slice of bread and a mug of water through a small opening near the floor. She grabbed the bread and was biting into it

[1]John 10:18

[2]John 1:29

[3]Romans 6:23

when she felt something crawling across her hand. "Weevils!" She brushed them off and threw the bread down in disgust. She stooped to pick up the mug of water, and since the knot of hunger was almost unbearable, she retrieved the bread and ate it with her eyes closed.

What had happened last night—was it real, or had she merely imagined it? Shivering in the dank cell, drinking water that smelled of sulfur, she decided it must have been a dream.

The door swung open and a guard jerked his thumb. "Out with you."

"But where are you taking me?" she asked.

"You'll see."

He bound her hands and led her through the streets. She feared that he was leading her to Smithfield to be burned, but instead he brought her to St. Paul's. She was taken into a room where five men sat behind a table.

"Widow Terrel—"

"Nay, I—" she tried to correct the name once more.

"Silence! You will get a chance to speak. Now, Widow Terrel, a complaint has been lodged that you have been illegally held and punished in the cage without a fair hearing. We, here, are the heresy commission duly appointed by the Bishop of London to try cases such as yours. We know beyond doubt that you are a messenger for the heretics." He held up Beatrice's letter. "This proves it. But we are not willing that any should burn if they but confess their sins, recant their heretical beliefs and," he poised a quill over a sheaf of paper, "tell us the names of the other misled followers of this false religion. Save yourself and the child you bear."

For a brief moment, Rose thought how easy it would be to yield, to give them names. After all, why should she sacrifice her unborn child for the lives of the London congregation? They had made their choices and knew the risks. Could she remember any names? She searched her mind, recalling the faces of the worshipers at the house on Pudding Lane, the little children, the apprentices, the older women—nay, she could not betray them at any cost.

Rose looked at the commissioners who were awaiting her answer and she felt panic rising up in her "Oh, God," she prayed, "are you truly with me?" The same peace that had come to her in the cell the night before swept over her now. He was with her, as near as if He were standing beside her with His hand upon her shoulder. Her voice was clear and firm as she said, "I will not betray my friends."

"Fool. Don't you know we have the power of life and death in our hands?"

As the commissioners conferred together in whispers, she looked about the room. To her left was a wall hanging depicting the resurrection of Christ. What had He said? "I am the resurrection and the life: he that believeth in me, though he were dead, yet shall he live: and whosoever liveth and believeth in me shall never die."[4] Had Derick been questioned in this very room; had he been comforted by remembering those words?

The head commissioner stood up and cleared his throat. "We have drawn up a confession for you to sign. I will read it to you:

Item one: That you did carry treasonous and heretical documents from abroad to England.

Item two: That you are a member of the unlawful conventicle in London.

Item three: That you do disdain the mass and abhor the Pope as the supreme head of the Church.

How say you to these charges?"

"They are untrue. I have told you that I simply carried a letter for a young girl. I am not a member of an unlawful group. As for the other, the mass and the Archbishop of Rome, I am a simple woman. I have always worshiped as I was told to worship, but—" she groped for the right words, "I never knew God. I never heard His voice or felt His presence in your church."

"Oh? And in which church have you found Him?" the head commissioner leaned forward.

"I have found Him in my heart."

"What pretty words," he said sarcastically. "What persons led you in this doctrine?"

She thought of Derick, of the humble believers who had secretly met in barns and houses, of Thomas. Finally she answered. "They who led me were those who shared their own simple faith in God, who relied not on ritual, but on the Word of God. They led me to it—and you also, my lord."

"What? You traitorous whore, how dare you accuse me of teaching heretical doctrine!"

One of the other commissioners snickered and said, "Tell us, how did he teach you?"

"He, all of you, did teach me by cruelly putting to death those whose only crime was loving God; by wrongfully imprisoning me and making me a gazingstock. For that I thank you. For if I had never seen your counterfeit religion for what it is, I might never have sought the true."

---

[4]John 11-:25-26

"Brave words for a wench on trial for her life and who must soon be delivered of a child. Recant your heresies and give us the names of your fellow heretics and it will go well with you."

"I have nothing more to say."

"Guards, convey her to Newgate Prison! Have the keeper put her on bread and water. She'll give us names soon enough."

Chapter Twenty

"THIRTY-THREE—" Rose reached under her pallet for the stick she used as a spoon and scratched another mark in the crumbling stone wall. "Thirty-four." Thirty-four days since the guards had dragged her down so many dark stairways that she felt as if she were entering the very bowels of hell, and had placed her in this small solitary cell in the depths of Newgate Prison. She stood up and walked the six paces to the opposite wall, her hand on her belly, waiting for the sign—ah, there it was, a little kick—the child still lived! "Thank you, Heavenly Father," she prayed. *Live, but for what fate?* a nagging voice whispered in her mind. Surely they would not kill her while she was still with child. She had heard an awful story from Beatrice when she was in Emden of a newborn babe being thrown into the flames along with its mother. "No, no, it will not happen. Think not," she told herself. "Your thoughts are never clear until you've eaten." She listened for the distant clang of metal which told her food was being brought.

At last a tin cup and a bowl were shoved through the opening in her door. Rose sniffed the contents of the cup. Cider. She dipped her makeshift spoon into the bowl. It was a watery soup with a bit of cabbage and a sliver of meat. She took her meager fare over to her pallet and forced herself to eat slowly.

'Twas a miracle—two weeks ago, when she thought she could not survive another day on bread and water, she had begun receiving ale or cider, and porridge or soup along with her ration of bread. She wondered if somehow Joan was responsible. Had she not said she was able to bribe the keepers of Newgate? Whatever the reason for the change in diet, Rose had gained a little strength back, and every day after she had eaten, she was able to think clearly for a while. She would first rehearse her replies to the commission in case

119

this was the day in which they would question her again. *I will be prepared this time,* she decided. She would answer their questions so skillfully that she would neither jeopardize her friends nor deny her faith in Christ. This time they would surely see she was innocent of any misdeed.

After this mental task was completed, she let herself indulge in her one pleasure. She thought back to her life in Boxton, to the little cottage and the smithy. She imagined that this child had been born, a son, and that Derick was still alive. She thought through a day, an ordinary day in their lives: she tending the child and cooking, Derick in the smithy, and then in the evening of the three of them sitting at table. Later, she tucking the child into his trundle bed and going into her bedchamber to Derick's waiting arms.

By nightfall, hunger gnawed at her again, and depression weighed her down. Often she prayed and the depression left, but she longed to learn more about God, to have someone with whom she could talk, to instruct her in the Word. She tried to remember verses she had read to Derick and bits of theology that had been discussed in Emden, but her mind often became confused. "Dear Lord," she prayed, "send me a cell mate, a sister in the Lord. If I must stay here alone any longer, I feel I shall go mad."

She had given up any attempt at keeping herself tidy. Her hair was full of lice, her gown was as filthy as the pallet on which she slept. *There is one blessing,* she thought with a wry grin—*for some reason the rats have not taken up residence with me. Mayhap they took one sniff and fled to a better lodging.*

On the thirty-sixth day, as she was just scratching the mark in the wall, the door swung open and two gentlemen entered the cell. "Phew!" one exclaimed as he held a perfumed handkerchief over his nose. "We cannot question her here. Bring her up into the air," he ordered the underkeeper.

Rose was taken into a small courtyard inside the prison walls. She looked up in wonder at the small patch of blue sky. "Keeper, take her back a few paces. She has brought the smell with her."

Rose blushed with shame. Here in the sunlight she could see the stains of vomit and excrement on her gown. *If I could have eaten before they questioned me; if they had allowed me to clean myself...* She felt weak and wretched.

"This is your last chance to answer correctly. Who were your accomplices in sedition and heresy? If you answer well, your life may be spared."

She remained silent. She knew she was too weak, too slow-witted from hunger to try to spar with them in conversation. She only wanted them to leave her alone, to take her away from their looks of disgust. She stood with her head bowed as they again read the list of charges against her.

"I've done no wrong," was her only reply.

"Very well, you are sentenced to be put to death by burning as soon as the child is born."

"My child!" She fell on her knees. "Please, don't let the child be harmed. What will become of it when it is born?"

"That is not for us to say," said one as he pulled on his gloves.

"She is to be placed in a condemned-prisoner cell," the other told the guard, and they both made a hasty retreat.

The new cell was large and, being just below street level, had two barred windows near the ceiling which let in air, cold but fresh. It was furnished with a table and two benches, a candle and a chamberpot.

For the next two weeks she was alone. Her back ached constantly, and her legs had begun to swell. One day the door opened and the keeper threw in a bundle containing a clean smock, a skirt and a comb. She recognized the comb, of tortoise shell in the shape of a fish. She had last seen it on the chest in Joan's bedchamber the night she was being fitted for the gown she would wear to Emden. So it was Joan who had arranged for better food! Just the knowledge that someone still cared about her warmed her heart on this freezing November day.

After she had changed into the clean clothes and was struggling to comb the snarls from her hair, the keeper brought in two women. One was about forty years of age. She leaned heavily on a staff, her fingers bent into unnatural positions as she gripped it. Her eyes held the look of someone in constant pain, but after the keeper had left, she turned to the other woman and said cheerfully, "Molly, praise to God, another sister to have fellowship with!" She hobbled over to Rose and extended her gnarled hand. "I am Elinore. What is your name, dear?"

As Rose introduced herself, she noticed the young girl, Molly. She was clad in a fine gown and lace-trimmed cap, from which bright auburn curls had escaped, framing her sad face. Molly was staring at Rose with a horrified expression on her face. "I—I know I must look dreadful," Rose murmured, "but 'tis so hard—"

"Never you mind," said Elinore. "We are glad of your company. Isn't that so, Molly?"

"Oh, why of course—forgive me," Molly said as she took Rose's hand.

Elinore carefully lowered herself down on a bench, an involuntary moan coming from her lips. "They made me stand so long during the questioning that I feared I would never be able to bend my knees again." She drew a small copy of the Scriptures from her bodice. "There's one advantage of having such a misshapen form. They never suspected that I had hidden this."

"Have you been sentenced?" Rose asked them, and then regretted her words as Molly began to weep.

"Oh, indeed," said Elinore briskly. "We are to die. On which day, we know not, but as I told his lord high uppity up, we will all die someday, and after that the Judgment, and woe to our persecutors in that hour! And you, Rose?"

"Aye, when the child is born."

"Hmph! The beasts have one drop of compassion, then."

Two days passed with no word as to when Molly and Elinore were to die. The next morning as Molly still slept, Elinore whispered to Rose, "I'll wager they are holding us until your child is born. Then we shall all be taken to Smithfield to be burned together. It makes a better show for them, you know, than if we were killed singly."

"What do you suppose will happen to my baby?"

"I know not, but God knows. He loves that babe more than you can fathom, and He will do what is best."

Rose silently thanked God for sending Elinore to her. Though her body was twisted, her faith was straight and true, and her confidence comforted Rose and strengthened her growing belief. Aloud she asked, "Elinore, have you known Christ long?"

"Faith, child, it seems I have had His fellowship forever, but 'twas eighteen years ago that I was reborn." She rubbed her hand. "This crippling disease came upon me of a sudden after I reached marrying age. Oh, I was a lusty wench 'til then. I could outspin, outdance, outlive any girl in my village. Then overnight I became wracked with pain, my joints so swollen that I could barely move. My true love did not remain true. He wished not to wed a cripple. I pitied myself greatly and decided to end my life one morning. I sought to drown myself in the river just outside our village. I struggled out of bed and hobbled down the lane. As I paused to rest in the market square, I heard a gospeller reading the Scripture, where Christ promises rest to the weary and heavy-laden. I gave my heart to Him right there. He forgave me of my sin, and although this disease is still upon me, His comforting presence has never left me. What about you—when did you trust Him?"

"I, well, I found Him—or rather He found me—in my prison cell." Molly had awakened, and she listened with Elinore as Rose told them briefly all that had occurred to bring her to prison.

"You're a babe in Christ!" Elinore exclaimed.

"Aye," Rose answered shyly. "I know so little."

"That may be true, but you do know the greater part, for you have already taken up your cross to follow Him.—Molly, 'tis your turn.—We but met in the room as we waited to be questioned," she explained to Rose. "Molly?"

The young woman nervously played with the ribbons on her gown and spoke so softly they could barely hear her. "My father and mother taught me in the way. One Sabbath last spring we were all at a secret service in the woods. The sheriff's men suddenly appeared and most of us scattered and hid among the trees. My mother was quite stout and could not run, so my father stayed at her side. I—I should have stayed, too."

"Nay," objected Elinore, "your parents would—" but Molly plunged on.

"I ran to a cousin's farm nearby, and he hid me in his hayloft. When no one came for me I kept to his house for weeks, never showing myself when strangers came. My cousin finally found out that my parents were going to be . . . were to die in a sand pit outside the village. I was so afraid, I did not even try to see them to tell them farewell on—that day." She wiped her eyes with her handkerchief. "But afterwards, another believer who knew where I was staying brought this." She drew a piece of paper from her pocket. It looked as if it had been folded and refolded many times. "This was written by my mother the night before her death." She opened the letter and read:

"Molly, my sweet daughter,

On the morrow, your father and I will take our leave of this world. In my mother's heart I am full of joy knowing that you will not suffer the fires with us. God willing, you will wed one day and bear children and tell them of the grandparents they will never know. Molly, dearling, as much as I hope for you to be spared any sorrow, I desire even more that you be true to Christ. He will be both Father and Mother to you now. I commit you to His loving arms.

Farewell,
Mother."

"How beautiful!" Rose exclaimed.

"Aye," Molly agreed, "and yet the letter torments me. Was I a cringing coward to run from the sheriff? I argued the matter with myself until I could bear it no more. One Sabbath morning I walked into church during mass and loudly cried out against all false worship. I was arrested, and here I am." She looked from Rose to Elinore. "Did I do the right thing?"

Elinore patted her hand. "Child, I've learned this: Even when we overstep God's best plan for us, He is able to work it to our good. You acted, mayhap, like young Moses when he went out to slay an Egyptian, overhasty to confront your enemy. But what's done is done. Rest in Christ now and let Him comfort you."

Molly nodded slowly. "If I had it to do again, I might not have run so easily to my imprisonment, but"— she thrust her chin up— "I'll not recant. Never!"

"Amen," Elinore said heartily. She held her gnarled hands out to the other two. "Sisters, let's thank God for His strength and loving-kindness."

Chapter Twenty-one

THE NEXT MORNING the keeper's wife entered the cell. She was a tall, spare figure, scowling from under thick eyebrows. She walked over to where Rose was lying and kicked her. "Up, wench!" she ordered. Rose awkwardly struggled to her feet. The woman looked her over from head to toe. "Turn around." Rose shot a questioning glance at Elinore and then did as she was told. "Mmm! you're sound enough of limb." She slapped Rose's protruding belly. "Its father, was he handsome?"

Surprised, Rose answered, "Aye, very handsome."

"Good. I'll take the child. My son's wife is barren"—she addressed the underkeeper who stood by the door—"and does naught but pine for a babe of her own. If she favors this one, 'twill give my son some peace. If not, I can sell it."

"You cannot take my child—I won't let you! Have mercy!" Rose clutched at the woman, but the underkeeper grabbed her and shoved her to the floor.

"Have a care," the woman warned him as she reached the door. "You'll harm the merchandise. Let me know when she's delivered."

As they left, Rose pounded her fists on the floor. "God, oh, God!" she cried. "Let not that awful woman take my child! My baby, my poor baby!"

Elinore and Molly helped Rose to the bench and put their arms around her as she sobbed.

"Mayhap—mayhap the child will not live, by God's mercy," Molly said timidly.

"Not live?" Rose laughed bitterly. "If you knew how many years I have longed for a living child, how his father dreamed of the day when he would have a son—" She looked around wildly. "This is a cruel jest of God's. I'm going mad."

Elinore held her tightly and began to pray, "Oh, Father, we know not what to ask, but, Lord, if it is your will, spare this child to be born. Lord, somehow keep it safe as you did the infant Moses when he was hidden in the bulrushes. Send a good woman to care for the child. We commit it to you. Amen."

Rose's sobs had turned into moans.

"What is the matter?" Elinore asked anxiously.

"I think—" Rose responded haltingly, " 'tis time for the baby. I have—" She winced and gasped a breath. "I have felt pains more and more frequently since late last night."

Elinore felt Rose's belly. " 'Tis time. 'Twill come quickly. Molly, help her to the pallet. Oh, I wish we had a bit of clean cloth!" Rose cried out in pain as Elinore sat down beside her on the straw. "These feeble hands.—Molly, tear a piece from my petticoat and wad it up. Now give it to Rose to bite on.—Try not to cry out, dear. We'll not have that wicked woman knowing any sooner than she has to. Why, what's this?" Molly had handed her a clean white smock.

"I was saving it for the day of my dying, but I want the baby to have it for its swaddling clothes."

After a few more hard pains, Rose gave a final muffled scream as the baby emerged. Elinore caught the child in her apron and instructed Molly how to tie off the cord with a strip from her smock. Then Elinore spanked the baby to get his lungs working, and after his first mewing cry, wrapped him in Molly's smock.

"Here he is, your little son. Put him to your breast and let him suck. 'Twill help stop your bleeding."

"A son, a son! Is he all right?"

"Aye, he is lusty. Now take him, dear."

Rose reached out for him and then withdrew. "Nay, I do not want to touch him. I love him so much—but he'll be taken from me. Oh, my heart is breaking!"

Despite her protests, Elinore laid the baby on Rose's breast. His little wet head turned, and his mouth started groping for food.

"Here, then, my little babe," Rose relented as she began to nurse him. She dried his head with a corner of the smock. "See how much hair he has! It is thick like his father's and just like his little brother who lived but a few moments. Oh, are you certain he is healthy?" Elinore nodded as she brushed a tear from her eye.

They heard a key turning in the lock of the cell door. Molly grabbed her cloak and threw it over Rose, concealing the baby. She stood in front of her and spread out her skirts so that Rose could not see the door, but she heard the creaking as it opened.

"A few minutes, mind you," she heard the underkeeper growl.

"A few minutes for all the money I gave you?" bellowed the visitor. "At least leave us alone."

It was Joan! Rose kept silent for fear the baby would cry. She waited until she heard the door close. As Molly stood aside she could see that Joan carried a large basket covered with a cloth.

Joan rushed over to her side. "Rose, are you ill? Oh, if you but knew how I've tried to get in to see you. That day, after I saw you in that terrible cage, I camped outside the Bishop's door insisting that you get a fair hearing. At least I tried to get these monsters who keep the prison to give you good food and clothing, but now you lie ill and—"

Rose had slowly cast aside the cloak, revealing the sleeping baby.

"Oh, praise be to God, you've got you a child! Just look at the precious—"

"Hush!" Elinore whispered, and hastily told Joan about the keeper's wife.

Joan picked up the baby. "She'll not have . . ."—she paused while she uncovered the child—". . . *him*," she finished. "Auntie Joan will protect him. Here—" She held the baby in one arm, and with her free hand emptied the basket she had brought of loaves of bread and a flask of wine. "We'll wrap him up, and I'll spirit him away in the basket."

"But what if he should cry?" asked Molly.

"I know what to do," said Elinore. "Molly, tear yet another piece from the smock and dip it in some of the wine." Molly did as she was told, and Elinore put the cloth to the baby's mouth and he began to suck contentedly. "My mother quieted my baby brother that way. 'Twill keep him still for a time, but hasten—the underkeeper may come back at any moment."

Joan gave the baby to Molly to hold as she knelt down beside Rose. Her tears fell on Rose's face as she bent to kiss her good-bye. "Would to God I could save you also."

"Just take care of my baby."

"I will, I will. I promise you he will lack nothing."

"His name is to be Derick. Tell him—tell him, when he can understand, that his father and I loved him very much."

"Quickly now!" Elinore urged.

Molly and Joan carefully swaddled the child in the smock and placed him in the basket. They had just covered him with the cloth when the door opened. "Time, madam," the underkeeper said, keeping his eye on the hallway. With a last glance at Rose, Joan hurried out. The door clanged shut, and the three woman held their breath as they listened for the baby to cry.

After a few minutes, Molly sighed and said, "They made it. Our little Moses is safe."

Later that day the keeper's wife came in and discovered that the birth had taken place.

"A curse on you, you ungrateful wretch!" she screamed as she showered Rose with blows. "I was going to save your child from being thrown into the fire along with you and this is how you repay me!" Elinore tried to place herself between Rose and the woman's fists, but she was pushed aside. "You've done nothing but hasten your death. I'll see to it that the authorities know of the childbirth to-day—and tomorrow you all will roast!" She left, and they heard her railing down the hall.

Molly helped Elinore to her feet, and together they went to Rose's aid. She was badly bruised but had no broken bones. Molly retrieved the loaves and the flask of wine which, in her rage, the keeper's wife had not seen. "Well, at least we shall feast tonight," she said as she placed them on the table.

"I've a better idea," said Elinore. "We have bread and we have wine—and this is to be our last night on earth. Tomorrow we shall attend the marriage supper of the Lamb. So now, sisters, shall we not celebrate the supper of our Lord?"

After Molly had helped Rose to the table, Elinore placed her hand on the loaf and said, "Let us take care to eat worthily. If we have hatred toward our persecutors, if there is fear or a drawing back from the suffering that is ahead, let us confess it to our Father." She paused while they searched their hearts. "If there is a looking back, a longing for the ease and pleasure of this world, let us renounce it also."

Rose thought of the baby she had held in her arms just a short while ago. "Thank you, Father, for sparing his life," she prayed.

"And now"—Elinore struggled to tear pieces of bread from the loaf—"here. Our Lord said, 'Take, eat: this is my body, which is broken for you.' "[1]

They ate in silence. Rose saw again in her mind the broken body of Christ as it hung on the cross. Her own sacrifice seemed so small.

Elinore held the flask of wine; as she passed it to Molly, she quoted Christ's words, " 'This is my blood of the new testament which is shed for many for the remission of sins. . . . This do ye in remem-

---

[1] 1 Corinthians 11:24, KJV

brance of me . . . till I come again.' "[2]

When it came Rose's turn to drink, as she lifted the flask, she spilled some of the red wine on her hand. She thought of the wonder that God's Son had poured out His life's blood for her. Here in this room the scent of blood was still strong, the blood that she had shed to give her son life. In her mind she saw the blood of Derick and all the martyrs flowing into that pure, godly stream begun so long ago.

Rose handed the flask to Elinore, but her gnarled hands were trembling, and she could not hold it. Rose helped her put it to her lips. Elinore drank and then began to weep. Rose and Molly were alarmed because they had never seen the older woman in despair.

After a while she said, "I am so sorry. 'Twas a passing weakness. After I said we should not draw back, Satan hurled his darts of doubt at me. I've disappointed you."

"Nay, dear friend," Rose said as she kissed her. "You have been our constant strength."

"Well, that shows you," said Elinore, composed again, "never rest your faith in aught but the constancy of Christ." She pulled her Bible out from under the pile of straw where she kept it hidden. "Rose, will you read to us tonight? And afterwards we shall put the Book back in its hiding place for the next believers who await their death."

Rose read far into the night by the light of the one candle. She read the joys of heaven; she read God's promises that He would never leave nor forsake His own, and how He had prepared a place for all His saints. She read until her voice was so hoarse that she could read no more. Elinore had fallen asleep after a while, but she and Molly were wakeful. She had her arm around Molly in the middle of the night when the girl suddenly asked, "Do you think it will take long? The burning, I mean. I never saw one. Will I look horrid before the fire consumes me?"

"Dear God," Rose prayed silently, "how can I give answer?" Finally she cleared her throat and said, "Nay, 'twill not take long. 'Tis the smoke that reaches you first. Breathe it in quickly and you will lose consciousness. Then you will not feel the fire." She stroked Molly's auburn curls. "And you won't be horrid. You will go to heaven in a blaze of glory, as fair as any bright angel."

Molly began to cry, "I love God, truly I do, but I want to live and wed and have babies. Oh, forgive me—I've saddened you. You must miss your baby so."

---

[2]Matthew 26:28; 1 Corinthians 11:25, 26, KJV

"There, there," Rose said, fighting back her own tears. "If we cared not to live, what sacrifice would it be to die? 'Twould be a small thing to run to the fire if we had no joys of living to lay down. Tomorrow, think not about what will happen at Smithfield. Think about the Eternal City, where there is no pain, no suffering, no tears. And think about the Lord saying, 'Well done, Molly, thou good and faithful servant!' " As Rose spoke, she felt Molly relax and soon fall asleep.

"Oh, Lord," Rose prayed again, "make them dispatch her speedily. Give me courage to be an example for her."

When light had filtered into the cell the next morning, and Elinore was moaning with the effort it took her to stand, a guard entered with a sheaf of paper in his hand. "Prepare yourselves. By order of Her Majesty the Queen, you are to be taken to Smithfield this day, tied to a stake, and burned until you are consumed. This is the writ of execution here ordered for Elinore Butler, Molly Cooke and Agnes Terrel."

"My name is not Agnes Terrel," Rose protested loudly. "My name is Rose Haler." If she were to die, it would be under her true name, and the surname that she had shared with Derick.

"What?" The guard hurriedly conferred with someone outside the door. "The Bishop and the commission are waiting. We will attend to you later. Stand aside," he ordered Rose as he led the two others out.

"We'll meet in heaven," Elinore called to her. Molly began to cry. "Chin up, Molly," Elinore's voice rang from the hallway. "This day we shall be with the Lord in Paradise!"

Chapter Twenty-two

"TAKE ME WITH THEM. I do not want to die alone. I'll go as Widow Terrel. Please!" She pounded on the cell door until her hands were bleeding, and then she slumped down to the floor. She waited beside the door for hours expecting them to return with her true name on a writ of execution, but when no one came, she crawled over to her pallet, wrapped herself in Molly's cloak and, clutching Elinore's Bible, fell asleep.

It was the middle of the night when she awoke to a sharp kick on her back. The keeper's wife was holding a candle close to Rose's face. "Why anyone would pay so much gold to spare your life is more than I can fathom. Get up!" When she arose, the woman caught Rose by the neck and dug her fingernails into her flesh. "If you want to stay alive, remember this: Your name is now Margaret Twillford. Never mention the names Agnes Terrel or Rose—"

"Haler."

"Whatever. Raph, bring the other one in." The underkeeper brought in something rolled in a rug. He dropped the bundle on the pallet where Rose had just been sleeping and unrolled the rug, exposing the body of a young woman. Her lips were pulled back from her teeth in a grimace of pain.

"How—how did she die?" Rose stammered.

"Fear not, we did not kill her to save you. Nay, 'twas the dank cell that did the job. She was raving mad with fever and would not take a sip of water for the last four days." She looked down at the corpse and then at Rose. "Mmm, the dead one's hair's too fair. Raph, rub some dirt into those golden locks. When they come back with a new writ, we want nothing to go amiss. You," she ordered Rose, "follow me, and count your blessings that you're more profitable to me alive than dead."

Numbly, Rose followed the keeper's wife up a staircase and to a small chamber that contained a bedstead, a small barred window at eye level, a table, and stool. "Coming up in the world, ain't you?" She grabbed Rose by the arm. "Say your new name."

"M-margaret, Margaret—"

"Twillford, Twill-ford!" She slapped Rose as she spoke and then pushed her onto the bed. "We'll get along nicely as long as the money from your friend flows in. If it stops—well, that's another story."

After she had gone, Rose rubbed her bruised face and tried to comprehend what had just happened. *I'm not going to die,* she thought in amazement. *I'm not going to be burned! Somehow Joan has bribed the keeper's wife to substitute that poor dead girl for me. I'm safe! Oh, no, poor Elinore and Molly—they've died, and I am spared because I have a rich friend. Dear Elinore, a thousand times better than I shall ever be—Molly, pretty as a flower, longing for a true love and marriage! Why, Lord, why have I been spared and they horribly killed?* She drew out the Bible that had been concealed in Molly's cloak. *I'm not good enough to be your martyr, is that it? Mayhap I am still a false professor.* She thought back to the night before when the three of them had observed the Lord's Supper. *Nay, I believe with all my heart—but still, why them and not me? Why me, here, safe, and not them?* She put the Bible under her mattress and tried to sleep.

In a few days her milk came in, milk that she could never give her child. Had Joan found a healthy wetnurse for little Derick? she wondered. Did she know the nurse must be honest, kind and wise, for these virtues would be passed from her to the babe as it suckled? "Oh, my baby," she cried, " 'twould have been better to die than to live out my days longing for the touch of his wet lips to my face!"

As the weeks passed, the Bible remained in its hiding place, for she could not bring herself to read it or to pray except to question her fate. Although this room was a hundred times better than the first dark cell she had inhabited, there was no difference to Rose, for the gloom of depression had settled around her.

Then one winter morning the underkeeper stomped in and threw a knotted napkin on her table. After he left she stared at the object a long while, then finally forced herself to get up from the bed and go over to the table. When she untied the knot a few crumbs of light bread spilled out from the napkin. *What else had the underkeeper confiscated?* she wondered idly. *Ah, he has left a few walnuts, a square of powdered beef wrapped in heavy paper—what is this?*

There was some writing on the underside of the wrapper. She

carried it over to the window and read it. "He laughed today." *Is that all? What could—* "Oh, Father in heaven—the baby laughed today! He is still alive and growing, and he laughed! Oh, thank you, God, oh, praise your name for sparing his life—and thank you for sparing mine! Forgive me, ungrateful wretch that I am." She hurriedly retrieved the Bible, and when she had found the page, read aloud, " 'For I am persuaded, that neither death, nor life, nor angels, nor principalities, nor powers, nor things present, nor things to come, nor height, nor depth, nor any other creature, shall be able to separate us from the love of God which is in Christ Jesus our Lord.' "[1] Death—nor *life*—He had spared her life for a reason. Mayhap she would never know it, but she silently vowed to live for Elinore, and Molly and Margaret Twillford—and for Him.

The months passed. Sometimes her faith was strong, and she studied God's Word and sang; at other times it seemed as if one gray day faded into another in an endless, hopeless march. Little pleasures magnified into big events: the day a redbird perched upon her windowsill; the first snowflake of the winter; the day a bit of yellow ribbon was carried into her cell by a whirlwind. After a while, she was allowed to exercise for an hour each day, the weather permitting, in the small courtyard where she had received her sentence of death. But her greatest joys were the brief messages Joan occasionally managed to send her. Just to know that the baby had taken his first step or had spoken a word brought tears of joy.

One dreary winter morning she lay abed with a wracking cough. "Two years I have survived," she sighed. "Not many have endured that long in Newgate Prison." She covered her ears. "Those bells again. Why this constant ringing of bells? Had Queen Mary finally borne a child?" She coughed and rolled over. "Why can they not let me rest in peace? I cannot last through another winter. Poor Joan— she must have spent a fortune keeping me alive all this time, and now I shall die after all."

She heard the key turn in the door but did not roll over. "Whatever slop you've brought me, I hope 'tis hot, I'm chilled to the—"

"Rose Haler?"

She sat up. A gentleman stood in the doorway with a sheaf of paper in his hand. Her heart began to pound. It had come at last— the writ of execution. She slowly got to her feet and looked around her cell. This small room that she had grown to hate now represented safety. Ah, well, she knew it would come someday. Fire or fever,

---

[1]Romans 8:38, 39

what did it really matter, the manner of her dying? She squared her shoulders and held her head up as she said, "I'm ready," and walked toward the door.

"Mistress Haler?" the man was watching her curiously. "Are you not going to bring your Bible?" She had forgotten to hide it last night and had left it on the table.

"I shall leave it for another," she said. "I see no reason it should burn with me in Smithfield."

"Smithfield? Oh, my dear sister—do you not know? Bloody Mary is dead and Elizabeth has been crowned Queen! All those imprisoned for opposing the Romish church are being released from their bonds!" He showed her the paper. "See, here is the order releasing you."

She looked at him in disbelief and then began to cry. The gentleman touched her shoulder. "Come now, you must hasten. Someone awaits you downstairs." She clutched the Bible to her breast and followed him down to the entrance of the prison. Joan was waiting in the street and embraced her.

"Oh, my dear, you look so pale and wan," Joan said as she threw a coverlet over Rose's shoulders. "Here, Alen," she called to her servant, "take her arm. We'll have you home in no time."

"Little Derick, is he well?" Rose asked after a fit of coughing.

"Hale and hearty. I thought it best that he wait for us at home. Oh, thanks be to our merciful sovereign, Elizabeth."

"Thanks be to God, who never left me nor forsook me," replied Rose, "and thanks be to you, my faithful friend—" She tried to say more but began coughing again.

"Here, we shall have plenty of time to talk when you are better. We're almost there—see the bridge in the distance?"

Rose could hardly see through her tears as they approached Joan's house on the bridge. She was tingling with excitement as Joan helped her into the parlor. There was a roaring fire in the fireplace, and seated on a rug before it were a maid and a chubby little boy playing with a ball. The firelight danced on his black curls as he reached out for the toy. In all her dreams of this moment, Rose had imagined swooping her son up and hugging him, but now she could only exclaim in wonder, "Oh, my son—my dear little son."

The child looked up from his play, smiled and rolled the ball toward her. She stooped to pick it up and then crumpled to the floor and sobbed. "I'm so filthy, I dare not touch him." She felt someone touch her head and looked up to see her child standing before her. His head was cocked to one side and he was frowning in concern.

Then he waggled a chubby finger and said, "No cryin'."

She grabbed him and held him tightly. He started to cry and Joan gently pried Rose's arms from him. "There, there, dear. 'Twill take a little while for him to know you. I'll put him down for a nap and fetch us some mulled cider."

Later, when Rose had bathed and changed into clean clothes, the two women sat before the fire. Joan told her how she had sent little Derick to her brother's house in York until she was certain that the authorities had accepted the corpse of Margaret Twillford as that of Rose Haler.

"God's hand of mercy was with us. I had gone to the keeper and his wife, offering whatever they asked if they would help you escape, when the underkeeper came in to tell them of the other girl's death. She had been languishing in prison on some minor charge and had no relatives, no one to care about her, and so the keeper's wife came up with the idea of switching your identities."

"It must have cost you all your wealth."

"Nay, not at all, but I would have paid it all gladly. I blame myself for your imprisonment. If I had not let you take my place as messenger—"

"The Exiles!" Rose suddenly exclaimed. "Since Elizabeth is on the throne, there's no need for them to stay in foreign lands. My brother—"

"Your brother, you found him, then? I had thought since you had returned to London that your trip had been for naught."

"I found him, and his wife," Rose answered. "Joan," she continued, "have you not been in touch with the Emden congregation? When will they be returning?" She joyed at the thought of seeing Robin again—and Thomas.

"I know not—the weather is poor now for sailing. After you were arrested, I trafficked no more in pamphlets and messages. The joy of the game was gone. I let the congregation think that it was you who died in prison." She saw the surprised look on Rose's face. "It was the child I was thinking of," she said defensively. "I had given you my solemn promise to care for the little lad. What if I had told them and one turned informer? How could I care for Derick if I was imprisoned?"

"You did well," Rose said soothingly. Could Robin or Thomas have known, then, that she had been imprisoned, and if they had learned it from some other messenger, did they believe that she died in Newgate? Ah well, she was free, and her son was asleep in the next room. She leaned back in her chair and closed her eyes.

Gradually her strength returned. She slowly took over the complete care of Derick until soon he was calling her "Mama" and sleeping in a little trundle bed beside her own. Joan forced all kinds of good food on her and watched over her like a mother hen. Rose had to insist upon being allowed to help Joan in the shop. One day when she looked at her reflection, she saw that except for shadows under her eyes and a lack of luster in her hair, she was much the same as she had been before her imprisonment.

In February she and Joan attended a Frost Fair. The Thames had frozen over and booths of all sorts had been set up on the ice. They were buying a stick horse for Derick when Rose gasped, "Could it be?"

"What is it?" Joan asked.

"Over there," Rose pointed to a crowd watching an acrobat. "That man in the russet cloak—he looks like Thomas, a man I—stay, let me catch up to him." She ran up to the man just as he turned around. It was not Thomas at all. That night and for many nights thereafter she dreamed of him. Sometimes the dream began with a scene in her cottage in Boxton. Derick would take her in his arms and then as she kissed him he would turn into Thomas.

By the time the ground had thawed and the trees were budding, Rose's life had fallen into a pattern. She grew listless and wished she had a place of her own where just the two of them, she and her son, could live. Joan had hired another steward. Hugh, it seemed, had run away with a scullery maid while Rose was imprisoned. This new steward, Alen, was a handsome, cocky young man, and Joan was much taken by him.

One afternoon they all strolled out into the suburbs beyond Bishopsgate. "Lizzie," Rose told the maid, "take little Derick out to run in the grass, but mind, don't let him near the archers." She turned to see Joan whispering something in Alen's ear and the steward pinching her cheek. Rose watched other couples strolling by and felt a pang of desire for married life again. She looked down the road she had traveled when first she came to London seeking her brother. "Joan," she called, "what day is this?"

"Why, April fifteenth."

Just two days before the anniversary of Derick's death. Three years ago. It seemed another life. She looked again down the road that led to Boxton. *Was it time?* she wondered. She turned to Joan. "If you can spare me from the shop for a few days, I need to make a journey."

"Why of course—but where are you going?"

"Into the past," she answered, "I'm going into the past."

Chapter Twenty-three

"DERICK, DERICK, little love, wake up. We're here." Rose lifted him from the bed of the wagon. The wagoneer Joan had hired for her stopped in front of the White Horse and helped Rose alight. She shifted Derick in her arms and wiped his face with her kerchief. "There, my little man, you want to look your best when you see Aunt Cecily and Uncle Chris." She carried him into the inn. Cecily had her back to Rose and was wiping a table.

Rose grinned and assumed a haughty voice. "Bring me cider— and serve it in a clean cup."

Cecily kept wiping as she answered, "All of our cups are—" she stopped and whirled around. "Rose, is that you? Oh, look at the pretty child! 'Tis a boy? I can never tell 'til they're breeched."

Rose nodded.

"Oh, I'm so happy for you." She peered at Rose's silken gown. "Aha, either your brother is quite generous or you have caught a rich husband."

"Nay," Rose said laughing, "I work for a mercer on London Bridge."

"Sit you here. You must tell me all that has befallen you, but stay.—Chris, Christofer!" she called. "Come and see our visitor and bring Rosie with you." She smiled at Rose. "Aye, I have borne a daughter since you left and have named her after my dearest friend."

"By my beard, I never thought we'd see you again!" Christofer charged into the room and pounded Rose on the back. He stooped down and tickled Derick under the chin. "What a sturdy lad. He'll have his father's shoulders for sure. When he grows up, I've a fair bride for him." Chris turned and took his year-old daughter from a maidservant's arms. He set her down on Derick's lap and both of the children began squalling.

"Let them be, Chris, you old bear," admonished Cecily. "Here, Nance," she told the maidservant, "take the children into the backroom so that we can hear ourselves talk."

Chris and Cecily listened with expressions that changed from joy to sadness as Rose told them of her life since she left Boxton. She sensed that they understood little of her conversion, but Cecily wept into her apron when she learned of Rose's long imprisonment.

When she finished, Chris shook his head sadly, "To think it was all for naught."

The words stunned her and she could not think of a reply as he continued. "Your imprisonment, Derick's death, all need never have happened. Look on it, Rose. In Edward's reign, we had the reformed religion, then for five years while Mary ruled, the Romish faith was brought back. Now, Elizabeth has decreed that we turn again. And so, you might well have remained as Cecily and I, drifting peacefully with the tides. Why, nothing of importance, except for the birth of our child, has happened to us since you left. Nay," he said as he folded his hand upon his ample belly, "the death or imprisoning of commoners makes little difference to the realm. 'Tis kings and bishops that order our faith."

As Chris was speaking, Rose thought for a brief moment that perhaps he was right, that it was all in vain, and then she realized the truth—if Chris had lived in Jerusalem long ago, he would have asked, "Why does the carpenter from Nazareth make so many enemies? Does not he know that 'tis the Pharisees and Sadducees that order our faith?" And when he saw this Jesus of Nazareth nailed to a cross outside the city, he would have shaken his head and murmured, "And to think it was for naught."

Cecily broke into the silence and changed the subject. "Did you ever think of us while you were away?" she asked Rose.

"Of a truth, I did, and I thought of Alice. The Queen's death must have freed her from her nun's garb."

"Aye," said Cecily, "and from her single life. Oh, it would have warmed your heart to see her reunited in wedlock with Barnabe! She had worn the somber nun's habit so long that she burst forth into a garb of varied hues. For her wedding she chose a russet gown with a saffron-colored apron—"

"And a cap with scarlet ribbons," added Chris. "The villagers thought she had gone mad. They had even begun to call her a looney last summer when she took to standing at the door of the church on the Sabbath and exhorting people to turn from the Romish ways. Imagine a nun trying to drive worshipers from the church!"

"She was always quoting Scriptures to me," laughed Cecily, "I blamed you, Rose. Alice told me that you had given her a copy of the Bible in English."

So Alice had been converted through reading the Scriptures for herself! Rose could hardly wait to tell her of her own conversion. They could rejoice together. "What did the Widow do about Alice's gospelling?" she asked.

"Nothing at all," said Cecily. "I suppose she had just enough family loyalty to refrain from turning her own sister in, but she must have reasoned that if she gave her enough rope, Alice would hang herself."

"Barnabe did fear for her safety," Chris chimed in. "She had been warned by the parson. If the Queen Mary hadn't died when she did—"

Rose stood up, "I must go see Alice."

"Oh, I—you couldn't have known," Cecily hesitated and looked to Chris for help.

"Alice died two months ago, soon after her wedding," Chris said in a low voice. "Her heart just gave out."

Rose sat down heavily. Alice dead—dear, motherly Alice, who had nursed her through childbirth and illness, and never turned away from helping anyone. She was silent for a moment and then asked, "How has Barnabe taken it?"

"A more sorrowful creature you've never seen," answered Chris. "Finally to have his Alice back and then taken away by death."

"And the shameful thing the Widow, her own sister, did," said Cecily.

"Aye," agreed Chris. "Since Alice had not been formally pronounced a heretic, they allowed her to be buried in the churchyard. Barnabe would have laid her to rest by the space saved for his own coffin, but the Widow insisted that she be buried in her family plot, and since the Widow was the church's largest contributor, the parson sided with her. It grieved Barnabe greatly; he sold all of his belongings and went to live with a brother in Norfolk."

"But not before he did the Widow in," whispered Cecily.

"Barnabe, a murderer?" Rose could not believe it. He had always been so gentle.

"Cecily, slander not our old friend," protested Chris.

"Rose, hear this," said Cecily in spite of his protest. "The fire which destroyed the Widow's home and burned her to ashes was set on the night before Barnabe left town. He was in here that evening, cursing the Widow roundly and drinking more than I had ever seen him drink."

"Well," said Chris, getting to his feet, "there's no use to gossip it about. The Widow is dead and Barnabe is gone—and I must get back to my customers. You're welcome to stay with us as long as you wish, Rose," he added as he left the table.

"Now to your plans," said Cecily. "Have you come back to Boxton to live?"

"Nay, I've come to say farewell."

"Farewell? But you just arrived."

Rose did not answer her. She could not put into words the need she had. Instead she asked, "May I leave little Derick with you for an hour or so?"

"Of course, but—" She watched puzzled as Rose hurried out the door down the lane.

Chapter Twenty-four

AS ROSE WALKED through the market square, several villagers watched her curiously, but no one spoke to her. Even had they thought her face familiar, never would they have believed that this fine lady, gowned in blue silk, was a former villager.

It was late afternoon, and the trees alongside the Green cast long shadows across the grass. The Green was deserted except for two little boys running after a floppy-eared brown puppy.

Rose searched for the exact spot but she could not find it. There were no more bare patches of scorched earth, just a lush growth of new grass. *Silly of me,* she thought, *not to remember that nature can easily cover the cruelties done to it.*

She waited while the children captured their pup and walked away. Then she said aloud, "Derick, I know not whether God allows you to hear my words. If not, I pray the angels will tell them to you. I understand now, my dearling. I understand all, because the life you found in Christ is now my life, also. We were one in wedlock, but now we are one in Him. You spoke truly when you said God would care for me and the child. We have a son. I have given him your name—and, oh, he is a fine lad! I will teach him of God's love and tell him of you and the others who spoke the truth of God and followed Him unto death. Farewell, my husband. When we meet again inside the gates of heaven, 'twill not be as man and wife but as brother and sister in Christ. So I say to the memory of our earthly life together: Farewell, my husband, my first love."

She breathed a sigh and waited with her head bowed. It was finished. The past had no more hold on her heart. She would always honor Derick's memory, but now, at last she felt free to love another. She turned her head. What was that sound? Hoofbeats?

"Rose—"

As she turned toward the setting sun she saw a man dismount and walk toward her. She shaded her eyes, trying to identify the figure silhouetted against the pink haze.

"Thomas!" Her heart jumped as she recognized him, and she ran to meet him. "But however did you find me?" she called.

He was grinning widely as he approached. " 'Twas no easy task. I recalled that you had mentioned living on London Bridge, and on the day I returned from Emden, I knocked on every door on the bridge until I came to Mistress Denley's. She sniffed me out like a bulldog until I assured her that I meant you no harm, and then she told me you had come here. I have ridden my poor horse almost to death this day. Luckily I inquired at the inn, and the innkeeper said you might be on the Green." He looked around, "Is this where your husband—?"

"Aye, near this very spot."

He laid his hands on her shoulders. "Mistress Denley told me of your imprisonment. Had I but known, I would have swum the North Sea and stormed Newgate to save you."

"I had a Savior," she said quietly. "Thomas, I'm a believer now. Christ has saved me."

"Praise be to God," he said as he took her hand. "You were ever in my prayers and my thoughts. When I returned from Frankfurt and you had sailed without a word, I knew you must not return my love."

"I—I was not then ready to give my love to you or to the Lord."

"I was so distraught, I returned to Frankfurt and plunged into the work, trying to forget you—but I could not." He was standing so close now, it made her tremble. She took a step backwards.

"Why, Master Stratton," she said coyly, "I would have thought you might have wed Beatrice."

"That woolheaded child? Nay," he said as he stepped closer to her, "I desired to wed a woman."

She looked away from his gaze. "I have changed. I am not comely."

"You are more than comely. You have a new loveliness."

Just the touch of his hand confused her thoughts. She tried to speak but stuttered, "M-my brother Robin, is he well?"

There was a touch of scorn in his voice as he replied, "Aye, he fares well, very well. He chose not to return to England to assist the reforming churches. He was offered a good position in Frankfurt and Mirabel convinced him to take it."

"Was their child born safely?"

"Twins it was—on the day after you left, Robin said. And their next was a son, and when I left for England they had another on the way."

Poor Robin, she thought, *he would have to acquire great wealth and hire many servants to wait upon Mirabel now or she would never let him have a moment's peace.*

"Speaking of children, Mistress Denley says you have a son. You must be very proud of him," Thomas said.

Ah me, she thought, *I could listen to that deep, melodious voice of his forever.* "Oh, indeed," she answered. "He's there at the inn."

"Rose—" He coughed and began again. "Rose, Elizabeth, our sovereign Queen, has restored to me all the lands which had been confiscated while I was in exile. I can provide handsomely for you and the child. I promise I will love him as if he were my own—not that I could ever take his fa—"

"I will."

"—father's place and—what said you?"

"I said, 'I will,' Thomas Stratton. I will be your wedded wife."

The two little boys had returned to play, and while their puppy circled the horse, barking and retreating, the boys laughed, pointing at the man and woman kissing on the Green.